THE JOHNNY COFFIN DIARIES

yeah, Im Johnny Coffin,
the greatest pimple on the planet

JOHN W SEXTON has had fiction and poetry published in most of the leading Irish literary journals, and is represented in several anthologies, the latest being *Poets for the Millennium*, edited by Ian Wild. His first collection, *The Prince's Brief Career*, was published in 1995. He is the scriptwriter for RTÉ Radio One's children's series 'The Ivory Tower', and has released a nine-track CD, co-written with legendary Stranglers frontman Hugh Cornwell, under the title *The Sons of Shiva*. When he was a kid he wanted to be an astronaut and live on the moon. He definitely didn't want to become a writer – because they always come to a bad end. However, the moon is a long way away and coming to a bad end isn't that bad after all, so now he's a writer.

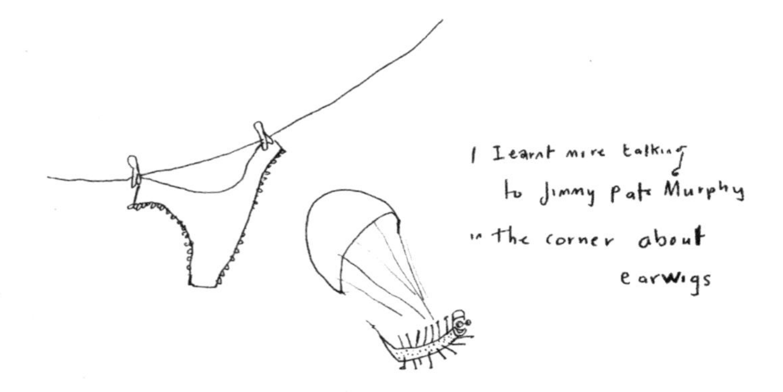

THE JOHNNY COFFIN DIARIES

JOHN W SEXTON

THE O'BRIEN PRESS
DUBLIN

Published in association with
RTÉ

First published 2001 by The O'Brien Press Ltd,
20 Victoria Road, Dublin 6, Ireland.
Tel: +353 1 4923333; Fax: +353 1 4922777
E-mail: books@obrien.ie
Website: www.obrien.ie

ISBN: 0-86278-704-1

British Library Cataloguing-in-Publication Data
A catalogue record for this title is available from the British Library

1 2 3 4 5 6 7 8 9
01 02 03 04 05 06 07

The O'Brien Press receives assistance from

The Arts Council
An Chomhairle Ealaíon

Layout and design: The O'Brien Press Ltd.
Author photograph: courtesy Peter Klein
Illustrations: Corrina Askin
Colour separations: C&A Print Services Ltd.
Printing: Cox & Wyman Ltd.

This book is for my youngest son
and wonderful assistant
Gerard

maths is the
language of the universe

CONTENTS

"Its a flying saucer sir!"

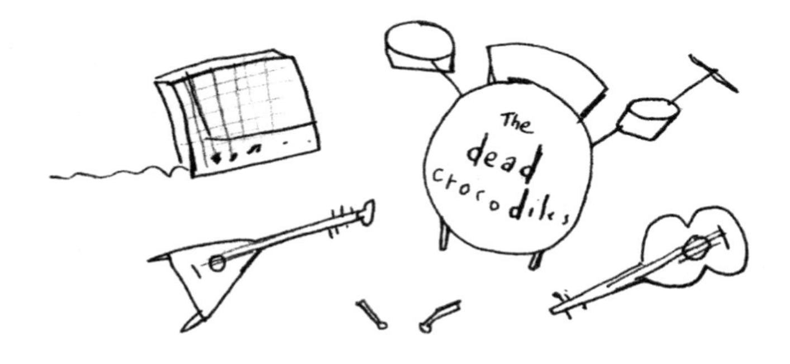
The dead crocodiles

let me introduce myself ...

My name is Johnny Coughlan, but everyone calls me Johnny Coffin because I have black hair and very pale skin and they say I look like a vampire. You probably think Johnny Coffin is a stupid name, but actually it's quite cool.

'Hey, there's Johnny Coffin,' people say, and those who don't know me think I must have killed somebody or something.

So I say to people, 'Yeah, I killed my teachers 'cos I didn't like them. I've killed two, but nobody can prove it.'

Sometimes I tell people, especially girls, that I'm called Johnny Coffin because I sleep in one.

'Yeah, right,' they say.

'No, I really sleep in a coffin. I have a cousin who's an actor and he was in a play called *Slime of Dracula*, and when the play finished he kept the coffin. He went to America and gave it to me before he left. But of course,

my Mam hates it.'

Or sometimes I tell them the truth – but not the real truth, but the truth that became the truth.

'I'm called Johnny Coffin because I'm in a band called The Dead Crocodiles.'

The thing is, I *am* in a band called The Dead Crocodiles. But we haven't played any gigs or anything: it's hard to get any gigs when everyone in the band is only twelve. And besides, Jimmy Pats Murphy, who plays lead guitar, is probably the worst lead guitarist in the whole world.

'So what do you do in this band?' people ask.

'I'm the drummer. My name is Johnny Coffin and I'm the best drummer in the world.'

Not a bad combination for a band: the best drummer and the worst guitarist in the whole world.

'Don't sweat,' says Jimmy Pats Murphy, 'I may be the worst guitarist in the world, but I'm getting better.'

And he'd get a lot better too, if only we had somewhere to practise besides my bedroom.

'*Will you shut up that awful racket*,' shouts Dad, '*you're destroying our brains*.'

Yeah, my name's Johnny Coffin. I'm twelve years of age. And I'm a dead crocodile.

i can defy gravity ...

I'm saving up to get a really cool pair of football boots. I've been thinking about them for weeks, and, you know, when you start thinking about new football boots you start to imagine that you'll begin to play better as soon as you get them. It's stupid, of course, because it's not true, but you imagine it anyway. So anyway, all this imagining must have been building up and building up inside my head, because last night I dreamt that I actually had these new boots.

We were in the changing rooms, and Monkey Murphy was shouting, 'Coffin Coughlan has some new boots, he might even be able to kick the ball this time,' and everyone was laughing.

But as soon as my boots were on I started to run all around the changing rooms. I was out of control. I couldn't stop. Faster and faster I was going, until finally I was running up the walls and all over the ceiling. Everyone was scattering in all directions, and

there I was, running up the walls and down the walls and couldn't stop.

Then I heard Mr McCluskey's voice: 'Coughlan, who gave you permission to defy gravity? Come down here at once, boy!'

And everyone was shouting, 'Coffin Coughlan's defying gravity', and the next thing I know, everyone is throwing apples at me, even my best friend Jimmy Pats Murphy. And as the apples hit me they go right through my body. I'm full of holes, and somehow I've slowed down and I'm on the ground.

Then Monkey Murphy throws an apple and it goes right through my head, and he's shouting, 'Look, sir, Johnny Coffin's got a hole in his head.'

Then Mr McCluskey is saying, 'Look at you, boy, you've got holes all over your body. You're in no condition to play, you're a disgrace. Get dressed at once.'

The team went on to lose five nil, and it was at that moment that I woke up.

So the match was a disaster and I never even got to play football.

But I still want those boots.

if a nine-year-old can do it ...

When I leave school I'm going to be a writer. Except at night, when I'll be playing drums in my band, The Dead Crocodiles.

At the moment I'm reading a book, a horror story about these two really wild characters who are trapped inside this building full of mazes and incredible rooms, and all kinds of weird creatures are running all over the place trying to catch them. It's called *The Ivory Tower* and it's written by the same guy who wrote *The Dead Crocodiles*. That's the book that gave us the name for the band.

Anyway, I'm reading this book and there's a knock on the door. It's my nine-year-old brother, Jerry.

'What're you doing?' he asks.

'I'm reading a book called *The Ivory Tower*.'

'Can I read it when you're finished?' he says.

'No, not until you're ten.'

So then he says, 'What's it about?'

So I tell him, and he says, 'If you're not gonna let me read it till I'm ten, then I'm going to go off and write my own story.'

He comes back half an hour later with a piece of paper written all over with pencil, in big loopy handwriting. He says, 'This is my story and it's called IN THE CASTLE. One night I heard a noise. Then a hole opened in the floor, and I fell into the hole. Then I found myself inside a castle. There was nobody there except all these ghosts who were going in and out through the walls. I was getting dizzy looking at them, going in and out through the walls, so I climbed the stairs to the highest tower. When I got to the top I saw a room. Inside were all these horrible wobbly monsters and they were having a party. I joined them and had a great time.'

'Jerry, that's the same story I just told you about,' I said.

Then Jerry says, 'So what? It's my story now, because I just wrote it,' and he leaves.

And that's what convinced me to be a writer: even a nine-year-old kid can do it.

And besides, at night I can still play the drums, and be *deadly* with the Crocodiles.

if aliens landed in the classroom ...

This morning Mr McCluskey said to the class: 'When aliens from outer space finally land on this planet, what language do you think they'll speak?'

For a few moments there was total silence, and we were all thinking: has Mr McCluskey gone off of his head? And *I* thought, maybe he has and they'll send us home.

Then Orla Daly stands up and says, 'Please, sir, they'll be speaking English.'

'Don't be stupid, girl,' says Mr McCluskey. 'They'll no more be speaking English than they'll be speaking Irish. But I'll tell the lot of you what they *will* be speaking. They'll all be speaking *Maths*, that's what they'll be speaking. And, Johnny Coughlan,' says Mr McCluskey, 'can you enlighten the class as to why aliens from outer space will be speaking Maths? And will you take your pencil out of your ear, boy, before

you puncture the few brains that you have left.'

'No, sir, I don't know why they'll be speaking Maths.'

'Of course you don't know,' says Mr McCluskey, 'well, sit down and I'll tell you. They'll be speaking Maths because maths *is the language of the universe*. And do any of you know why maths is the language of the universe? I'll tell you why,' says Mr McCluskey. 'Maths is the language of the universe because words are different for different people, but *numbers will always stay the same*. And let me tell you something else: if aliens from outer space were to land in this classroom at this very moment, not one of you would be able to understand them, because you are all sideways and backwards and upside-down when it comes to maths.'

Then Mr McCluskey turns around and draws something on the board, and he says: 'Mickey Murphy, please enlighten the class as to what this is.'

So Monkey Murphy stands up and he looks at the board and he says, 'It's a flying saucer, sir!'

'No, boy, it is *not* a flying saucer,' says Mr McCluskey, 'it is an *isosceles triangle*.'

And that is what we learnt at school today: how to talk to aliens.

worms are easy ...

'Did you write your essay on worms?' said Jimmy Pats Murphy before the start of school this morning.

'Oh no! I forgot. Mr McCluskey will kill me for sure this time.'

'Don't worry,' said Jimmy Pats, 'worms are easy. Didn't I write my own essay on the bus this morning. Lucky we stopped at three traffic lights.'

'But I didn't even read anything,' I said, 'What do I know about worms?'

'There's nothing to know,' said Jimmy Pats. 'They *live* in the ground and they *eat* the ground. Look, it's simple. I'll tell you what to write. And every few sentences just repeat what you've said in slightly different words. Before you know it you'll have written a page.'

'I don't know what you mean,' I said.

'Don't *worry*,' said Jimmy Pats, 'just start writing

every word I say.'

So I start writing down every word that Jimmy Pats says: *Up to three million earthworms live in an acre of ground. They are a most abundant creature, digging holes that are six feet deep. They eat large amounts of soil, digesting the bacteria and all the other germs. They help dig up the ground and keep it fresh. If a bird eats a bit of a worm, the worm will grow again, but if a bird eats half a worm, the worm will die.*

'Is that it?' I said.

'Yeah,' said Jimmy Pats. 'Now all you have to do is keep writing the same thing all over again in different words, until you get to the bottom of the page.'

Well, the way Jimmy Pats was saying it, it sounded simple enough, so that's exactly what I did. However, during the first lesson I discovered that things are *never* simple.

'Tell me, Johnny Coughlan,' said Mr McCluskey in his most sarcastic voice, 'has your entire family recently moved house?'

'No, sir.'

'And you're absolutely certain that you haven't taken up residence in an echo-chamber?'

'No, sir.'

'That's strange,' said Mr McCluskey, 'because there's an *inordinate* amount of *repetition* in your essay on *worms*. Can you explain this, Johnny Coughlan?'

'No, sir.'

'Well, boy, I can see by your replies and by this masterpiece of an essay, that you are an expert on repeating yourself. So perhaps tomorrow morning I could have an essay on *repetition*.'

'Don't worry,' whispers Jimmy Pats, 'I'll help you to write it.'

Yeah, thanks for nothing, Jimmy Pats Murphy.

welcome to the Planet of the Murphys ...

Today a new boy joined our class, and Mr McCluskey introduced him. 'This is Dinny Murphy,' said Mr McCluskey, and he gave us all a stern look, because he knew that we all wanted to burst out laughing. Poor Dinny Murphy was looking around the class at everybody, and I could see that he imagined that we had something against him, that maybe we thought he was stupid or something. It wasn't until first break that he found out the real reason.

'So you're a Dinny Murphy then?' said Monkey

Murphy to Dinny Murphy in the yard. A whole crowd of us had gathered around, and Dinny Murphy was looking very worried.

'Relax,' said Monkey Murphy. 'What do you think I am, a psychopath or something? Do I look dangerous? Well, I'm only dangerous if people annoy me. You're not going to annoy me, are you? I get really mad if people annoy me. No, it's no good. I'm sorry, you're beginning to annoy me already.'

'Why! What have I done?' said Dinny Murphy.

'Well, it's very simple,' said Monkey Murphy. 'You see, your name's Dinny Murphy. Actually, we have a Dinny Murphy already, *and* a Din Murphy, a Dan Murphy, a Danny Murphy, and a Don Murphy. That's why everybody around here has a nickname. Like, Dinny Murphy is Skinny Dinny, because he's so fat, and Din Murphy is Fat Murphy because he's so skinny, which is kind of mad. I mean, just thinking about this stuff would give you a brain tumour. And Dan Murphy is called None Murphy because he's so dull, and Danny Murphy is called Dense Danny because he's so thick. As for Don Murphy, he's called something as well, but I can't remember what it is. But the whole point is this: it's already confusing enough without getting another Dinny Murphy. And when I get confused I get annoyed.'

'Well, you can call me something else then, if you want,' said Dinny Murphy, trying his best to be helpful.

'You can give me a nickname just like the others.'

'Yeah,' said Jimmy Pats Murphy, 'why don't we call you Manky Murphy, to distinguish you from Monkey Murphy?' At that point Monkey began to chase Jimmy Pats down the yard.

'When I get hold of you, Jimmy Pats, I'm going to kick your brains over the cross-bar,' screamed Monkey.

But it was far too late for such flamboyant football skills, because everybody liked the name and so Dinny Murphy was christened Manky. To distinguish him, of course, from Monkey.

'Hi, my name's Johnny Coffin,' I said to the new kid. 'Welcome to the Planet of the Murphys.'

But before I could say another word Mr McCluskey was banging on the staff-room window and screaming at Monkey: '*Murphy*, what the hell do you think you're doing, boy?'

Everyone in the yard turned round. Well, everyone except *me*, that is.

Albert who??? ...

'*Johnny Coughlan*,' screamed Mr McCluskey from behind his desk, 'have you by any chance been taking English grinds from Albert Einstein?'

'No, sir,' I said, desperately trying to think who Albert Einstein was.

'Well, boy, there seems to be an *inordinate* amount of *time travel* in this composition of yours!'

'Excuse me, sir?'

'*Time travel*, Coughlan, *time travel*,' screamed Mr McCluskey. 'Your tenses, boy, are going backwards and forwards in time as if they are caught in a *time warp*!'

Mr McCluskey had his back to the blackboard, which was milky with chalk, and he looked as if he was surrounded by a halo. But I couldn't imagine what kind of heaven *he* could come from.

'Listen to this sentence, boy!' Mr McCluskey began to read from my composition:

‘ *“The old woman picks up the dead frog by one leg. She didn’t mean to kill it. It was the fault of the lawnmower, she thought.”* ’

Then Mr McCluskey said: ‘Can anybody tell me what is wrong with this sentence?’

Monkey Murphy stands up and says: ‘Yes, sir. The old woman shouldn’t blame the lawnmower. Lawn-mowers can’t kill frogs, sir, because they don’t have free will.’

‘*Murphy*,’ screamed Mr McCluskey, ‘this is an *English* lesson, not a *Theology* lesson. SIT DOWN, BOY! Well, Coughlan, what have you got to say for yourself?’

‘Well, sir,’ I says, ‘she *picks* up the frog because it’s happening *now*, but she *blamed* the lawnmower, because that’s happening *then*.’

Mr McCluskey looked me straight in the eye and his face went purple. ‘SIT DOWN, COUGHLAN, and do it NOW, not THEN!’

Mr McCluskey obviously needs to take some English lessons. Maybe he should talk to this Alfie Einstein.

like I'm the Green Lantern ...

As I told you, our school boasts the best collection of Murphys to be found anywhere in the whole country, and the most exotic of them all must be the three John Murphys. First of all, there's John Murphy, who, to reduce confusion, is simply called John Murphy. Then there's the second John Murphy who's known as Murphy, and the third John Murphy who's called Murphy-Murphy. Now, as it happens, Murphy-Murphy is a first cousin to John Murphy, the first Murphy, but Murphy, that's the second Murphy, isn't a relation of either of the two Murphys (although he is a second cousin to Monkey Murphy, not to be confused with Manky Murphy).

Anyway, of all the three John Murphys, the most interesting is Murphy-Murphy on account of the fact that he's always dreaming. The reason he's always dreaming has probably a lot to do with the fact that he's always sleeping.

'You, John Murphy, wake up, boy!' screams Mr McCluskey. And none of the other John Murphys looks up, because they *know* he can mean only *one* John Murphy.

'Do you know something, Johnny Coffin,' said Murphy-Murphy the other day, 'I sometimes wonder if I'm ever awake at all. Maybe *everything* is a dream.'

'Well, Murphy-Murphy,' I said, 'maybe you could wake up from this dream of yours, so that I could go home.'

'Nah, Johnny, I'm being *serious*. I even think that I'm on the Earth to serve a *special purpose*.'

'Yeah, yeah, like to spend your whole life being asleep. Get real, will ya!'

'Nah, I'm telling you, Johnny, while I'm asleep it's like I'm *protecting the whole world*. It's like I'm the Green Lantern or the Incredible Sleeping Man. Every night for the past week I've been dreaming of this guy with dark glasses entering my room, and when he takes off the glasses beams of purple light come out of his eyes and go into my *brain*. And then I wake up. He's obviously an alien or something, and he's trying to steal *all my dreams*.'

Yeah, I'm thinking, *Murphy-Murphy is completely off his head*. Then I see Mr McCluskey is looking over at us, so I pretend to work on my essay. But it's too late.

'Murphy and Coughlan, you boys, wake up, you're dreaming!' shouts Mr McCluskey.

The terrible thing is, we're *not* dreaming, we're wide awake.

it had turned green ...

This morning at breakfast my brother Jerry says: 'What ... what's wrong with the end of your nose?'

'Shut up, will ya. There's nothing wrong with the end of my nose.'

'But ... there's a big red spot on your nose. I can see it.'

'Jerry,' I said, 'shut up or you'll be seeing big red spots in front of your *eyes*.'

Then in the schoolyard Jimmy Pats Murphy says: 'Wow, Johnny, that's an amazing spot. Where'd ya get it?'

'I got it at the end of my nose, you eejit. Now, *shut up about my spot*!'

The rest of the morning seems to be going well, until Mr McCluskey shouts at the top of his voice: '*Johnny Coughlan*, stop picking at your nose, boy! It's *algebra* we're picking at today, Coughlan! *Algebra*!'

And of course, everyone turns around to look at my nose, and I can feel it getting hotter and hotter!

'Hey, look at Johnny Coffin,' sniggers Monkey

Murphy, 'he's got a *lighthouse* on the end of his nose.'

If this wasn't bad enough, it got worse. After the lunch-break I noticed that it had turned green. I was in the toilets looking at it in the mirror, getting ready to pop it, but I couldn't, because Monkey Murphy had come in and was watching me.

'Hey, Coffin,' says Monkey, 'you don't need to look in the mirror. Just look down your nose, you can't miss it.'

Back in the classroom I decided that I would probably survive the rest of the day. I mean, there were only a few hours left. Then it happened.

'Hey, Johnny,' says Julie Hegarty, and I look up and see that for the first time in my life, for the very first time in my earthly career, Julie Hegarty, the deadliest, most beautiful girl in the history of mankind, is actually talking to *me*.

'Yes, Julie?' I say, and I have totally forgotten that my face is hideous, that my life is over. And once again I'm Johnny Coffin, the coolest dude on the planet Earth.

'Johnny,' says Julie, 'have you a spare pencil?'

Then Monkey Murphy says: 'Now, don't forget to give Coffin back his pencil when you're finished, Julie. He might need it ... to burst his spot.'

Yeah, I'm Johnny Coffin, the greatest pimple on the planet Earth.

Dad actually knows something … not!

So I'm pouring out the cornflakes, hearing them go rattle-rattle-rattle into the bowl, and Dad's sitting with his face behind the paper, giving me advice on football: 'Now, son, what you need to learn is how to *communicate* with the ball,' and every now and then I'm answering 'Yeah, yeah' and 'Right, Dad, you're right, Dad,' but I'm not really listening to a word he's saying, because I know he hasn't a *clue* what he's talking about.

Then Jerry walks into the kitchen and he says, 'Dad, can I ask you a question?' and Dad says, 'Sure, son, you can ask anything you want,' and I just know that it's going to be one of those *stupid* questions that nine-year-old brothers are *always* asking.

So Jerry says, 'Dad, how come people can't talk if their tongues get cut off?'

Then Dad says, 'Well, Jerry, it's very simple,' and I'm

starting to think to myself, no, Dad, please don't try to answer this *stupid* question as if you know what you're talking about. But it's too late because Dad has already started.

'Well, Jerry, you see, the mouth is like a musical instrument and you make sounds by passing air through your mouth just like you would if it was, say, a tin whistle. Now, if you blew through a tin whistle you'd get music, but if you blew through a tin whistle without moving your fingers over the finger holes you'd only get a sound like a noise, and it *wouldn't* be music. To get music from a tin-whistle you have to use your fingers as well as blowing into it. Well, it's the same with your mouth. If you didn't have a tongue you'd still be able to make a noise, like a grunt or something, but you wouldn't be able to make words. So your tongue is just like using your fingers on a tin whistle.'

And all the time that Dad is talking I'm thinking to myself, hang on a minute, Dad is actually making *some sort of sense*. Dad actually *knows* something about something.

So I say, 'Dad?' and Dad says, 'Yeah?' and I say, 'Well, Dad, about this *communicating* with footballs, how do you actually do it?'

'Well, Johnny', says Dad, 'it's like this. Most people think that a football is an *inanimate* object, but actually it isn't, because it's acted upon by the *conscious mechanical efforts* of other people ...' and while Dad's speaking I'm beginning to say, 'Yeah, yeah,' and 'Right, Dad, you're right, Dad,' but I know that it was only a *fluke*, and that Dad really hasn't got a *clue* what he's talking about after all.

there's these massive tadpoles ...

So I'm in this dream, but of course I don't realise it's a dream. I just think it's real life, and I'm walking into the classroom after the break. Everybody else is already at their desks, but when I look up I see this enormous glass jar full of water in front of me, beside the blackboard, and it's as big as a *wardrobe*. When I look into it I see that there's these massive tadpoles swimming about inside it. I mean, *massive*, like, they're the size of fish. And as I'm looking I see that they have *human heads*. I see one with Jimmy Pats Murphy's head, and one with Monkey Murphy's head, and one with *my* head. Then I hear Mr McCluskey shouting: *'What are you doing, Coughlan? Sit down, boy!'*

'But, sir, these tadpoles, sir, they've got our faces, sir!'

'*Of course they've got your faces, boy!*' screams Mr McCluskey, as if it's the most normal thing in the world. 'They've got your faces because they're the new *class*. And when they're fully grown, I sincerely hope they won't be as dopey as you lot. Now, *sit down, Coughlan!*'

So I sit down, and I notice that everybody's busy working, with their heads down in their books. Then Jimmy Pats Murphy looks up and I see that he's a ... that he's *a zombie*! The *whole class* are zombies!

'*Johnny Coughlan*,' screams Mr McCluskey, 'stop looking about the place and do your work!'

So I pretend to do my work, but I notice something out of the corner of my eye. And when I look up I see that it's Murphy-Murphy.

Murphy-Murphy has fallen asleep at his desk and he's begun to float in the air. And I'm thinking, if Mr McCluskey sees Murphy-Murphy floating in the air, he'll know he's fallen asleep, and he'll start giving out. So I start whispering, '*Murphy-Murphy, wake up, wake up!*' But Murphy-Murphy's head flops to one side, and I notice that his ears are as big as buckets. And suddenly balls of paper start to fall out of one of his ears. And the paper keeps falling and falling, until we're up to our knees in paper. And nobody notices because they're all zombies. I pick up a piece of paper and written on it is this stupid dream that we're in. And the writing ends at the bit where I pick up the piece of paper. So I pick up another piece to see what happens next, but it just says the same thing. There's millions of sheets of crumpled paper coming out of Murphy-Murphy's ears, *and they all describe the same thing*! Then all I can hear is Mr McCluskey screaming, '*John Murphy*, stop that *floating*, boy. Wake up, boy! *Wake up, wake up, WAKE UP!*'

And that's when *I* woke up.

how can you tell if a moth is left-handed? ...

Because Jimmy Pats Murphy had designed the most perfect paper-airplane in the history of aviation, and because this airplane had circumnavigated the classroom and finally landed in Mr McCluskey's left ear, we found ourselves standing in two separate corners of the classroom during the first break.

'Hey, Johnny,' said Jimmy Pats, 'is there anything

exciting happening over in your corner?'

'Ahh, will ya shut up, you *dope*. It's all your fault that I've got to spend the break in this stupid corner in the first place!'

'Nah, Johnny, I mean, is there anything interesting happening? 'Cos in my corner I've got the most *amazing* moth. It's *left-handed*.'

'Will you ever get real! How can you tell if a moth is *left-handed*? Anyway, they don't have hands, they have wings.'

'Don't be stupid, Johnny. I can tell it's left-handed because it's using its left wing more than its right. The trouble with you, Johnny, is that you think insects are just insects.'

'Jimmy Pats, what the hell are you talking about? Of course insects are just insects. What else would they be?'

But of course, Jimmy Pats was ignoring the question, and had launched off on one of his bizarre lectures.

'Take earwigs, for instance. I've often found them curled up inside my Mam's clothes pegs, up on the washing-line–'

'Ah, pull the other one, Jimmy Pats, you couldn't even *reach* the clothesline!'

'No, I'm serious. Have you ever wondered what earwigs are doing inside clothes pegs? Have you ever even wondered how they got there in the first place?'

'Listen, Jimmy Pats, the only thing I'm wondering about is why I'm looking into the corner of this wall and listening to you!'

'Your problem, Johnny, is that you never wonder about things. Let me tell you something about earwigs. First of all, they *don't* climb inside people's ears, and they *don't* eat people's brains. That's just a load of rubbish. But what most people don't know is that earwigs have *wings* and they *fly*. It's just that hardly anybody sees them do it. Their wings are folded up very small inside their bodies, like a parachute. And, with wings that small, they can't take off from the ground, so they climb up to a high place, like somebody's clothesline, where they'll curl up inside the clothes pegs. Then the following night, when they want to go about, they just fall out of the clothes pegs, open their wings and fly like a glider. When they land they use their pincer-things to fold up their wings again, and tuck them back inside their bodies. And *that's* why you find them inside *clothes pegs*. And if you want to know my honest opinion, I don't know why people don't keep earwigs as pets. I mean, you could even keep one in your pocket.'

Now, the point is, when I got home I looked up earwigs in the encyclopedia, and do you know something, all that stuff that Jimmy Pats was blathering on about is actually *true*. Which means I learnt more today standing in the corner listening to

Jimmy Pats Murphy than in a *whole week* of listening to Mr McCluskey.

this is the voice of the Incredible Sleeping Man …

Dear Diary, because you have no brain of your own you're just going to have to believe every single thing I write down. And anyway, it's all *true*.

Firstly, Murphy-Murphy wasn't in school today. Secondly, Mr McCluskey was standing by the blackboard, and he'd handed me a piece of chalk, and I could hear his voice blaring over my head:

'Now, Coughlan, perhaps you could tell us the length of the hypotenuse at x if the other two sides of this right-angled triangle are *three* and *two* respectively. And just to make things easy for you, boy, it's a *right-angled* triangle, which means we can apply the theorem of Pythagoras, who, as we know … blah … blah … blah … '

It's at that point that my mind *went completely blank*

and all I could hear was 'Blah ... blah ... blah ...' and I knew Mr McCluskey was going to blow his top when he saw that I wasn't listening. But I couldn't help it, I'd just gone into a *daze*. And that's when I heard it ... that's when I heard the voice of Murphy-Murphy ... *right inside my head*:

'Johnny Coffin, this is the voice of Murphy-Murphy, the Incredible Sleeping Man ... I am talking to you through a telepathic link directly to your brain. The reason that I can talk to you is that your mind has gone completely blank because you are trying to learn maths. You must come to the Ivory Tower and rescue me. I have been kidnapped by Mr Darkness. The future of the Universe is in your hands.'

So, I'm starting to think, let's get this straight: Murphy-Murphy is trapped in a *novel* and he's sending *telepathic messages ...*

'Coughlan, COUGHLAN!' screamed Mr McCluskey, 'Coughlan, have you heard a single word I was saying?'

'Yes, sir,' I said, lying hopelessly. But then I started to hear that voice again, inside my head, the voice of Murphy-Murphy:

'Johnny, if you help me, then I'll help you. This is the answer to the sum. Repeat it after me.'

So I started to say, in my loudest voice:

'Ah, Mr McCluskey, this is *easy*. The square of *x* is equal to the *sum* of three squared plus two squared, which is ... *thirteen*. And the *square root* of thirteen is three-point-six, so *x* must be three-point-six. Really, sir, it's quite straightforward.'

Well, by the look on Mr McCluskey's face, I could tell that *I had actually got the answer right*.

But that was the easy part. *Now I've got to save the whole stupid universe*.

Professor Bang made a deal with Baby Chaos …

This morning I went to school and decided, *today is going to be normal*. I'm not going to talk to Jimmy Pats Murphy, he's mad. I'm *definitely* not talking to Murphy-Murphy, and I don't *care* if he needs my help to save the world. And I'm going to avoid Monkey Murphy at all costs, because he's a psycho. I'm just going to think normal thoughts all day long.

And everything was going fine, until half-way through the first class.

'*Coughlan*! Stand up, boy!' screamed Mr McCluskey.

'Yes, sir,' I said, determined that today was going to be a new beginning in the life of Johnny Coffin.

'As you have so obviously been listening to every

word I've just been saying, you can demonstrate the difference to the class.'

But of course, I didn't have a *clue* what Mr McCluskey was talking about, because I *hadn't* been listening. I'd been *thinking*, thinking about how *normal* things were going to be.

'The difference, sir? What difference, sir?'

'The difference between fact and fiction, boy! Now, as you are so alert, you can demonstrate *fact*. Tell us about your *week*. Come on, boy, make it quick.'

Now, the problem is, my week was kinda busy, because I managed to save the entire universe. Of course, if you blinked, which no doubt you did, you'd have missed it, which no doubt you did, because it happened in *a parallel universe*.

Anyway, without thinking of the consequences, I told the *facts*. 'Well, sir, it started with Mr Darkness, the most evil entity in the entirety of existence, when he kidnapped Murphy-Murphy and took him to the Ivory Tower, which, as you know, is a novel ... so Professor Bang, the greatest mind in the Universe, zapped me into my computer and transferred me into the novel as a word-file. But this guy with two heads, called Baby Chaos, had messed up the punctuation so I got stuck behind a dozen full stops. And Professor Bang had to make a deal with Baby Chaos so that we could get back, and that's why I was able to come to school this morning, sir.'

There was complete silence, and I suddenly realised that I was about to die. But instead, Mr McCluskey said: '*Excellent,* Coughlan, *absolutely* excellent!' And he turned to the class and said, 'By the use of *paradox* Coughlan has demonstrated *fact* by giving us *total fiction*. Sit down, Coughlan, you've obviously been paying attention after all.'

So I sat down, totally mystified, because I didn't even know what a paradox was. But the thing is, because Mr McCluskey seemed to know what it was, that's all that counted. And then I realised that as long as everything was *normal* nothing would *ever* be normal.

And, for all I know, maybe even *that's* a paradox.

his head looked like a giant blister ...

Barry O'Flynn, the bass guitarist in our band, The Dead Crocodiles, had just had his head completely shaved.

'Hey, Johnny, what do ye think of me new hairstyle? Isn't it *cool*, don't I look really *hard*?'

'Yeah, Barry, you look hard all right. Like a hard-boiled egg.'

'Hey, will you look at Flynn,' says Monkey Murphy. 'His head is like a giant blister.'

Well, that was it! From that moment Barry was renamed Blister O'Flynn.

Now, for some reason that I couldn't figure out, Jimmy Pats Murphy thought this was great. He just couldn't stop talking about it.

'Nah, Johnny, you just don't get it. Listen, this is going to be great for The Dead Crocodiles.'

'Jimmy Pats, what the *hell* are you talking about?'

'Johnny, you're so thick! Look, it's a great name for someone who's in a *band*. We've got Johnny Coffin on drums and Blister O'Flynn on bass. Now we're like a proper rock 'n' roll band.'

'Yeah, yeah, get real, will ya! And what about you? Oh, I know. We can call you ... *Cow Pats Murphy*.'

'Oh, very funny. Anyway, there's always *someone* in a band with a *sensible* name. So I was thinking of calling myself James *P* Murphy.'

'Nah, I've got a better one. How about James *Pea-Brain* Murphy?'

'I'm trying to be serious here,' said Jimmy Pats. 'If The Dead Crocodiles is to have a future we have to have proper names. Especially when we go on tour.'

'How can we go on tour, you lame-brain? We can't even get a gig.'

'Well, I've been thinking about that, and that's why I think we should go *busking*. We can do it over the holidays. We'll make a *fortune*.'

'Ahh, you dope! How can we go busking with a rock 'n' roll band? I can't take a drum kit onto the street!'

'Nah, Johnny, we won't go as a rock 'n' roll band, we'll go as ordinary buskers with two acoustic guitars, and you can play the *bodhrán*. We'll do traditional stuff.'

'Hey, get out of that, Jimmy Pats Murphy! *I'm a Dead Crocodile*. I'm not playing leprechaun music on a dead goat!'

Man, that Jimmy Pats Murphy! Next they'll be calling us The *Bog* Crocodiles.

it looked like a flag of crystallized bogeys ...

Today in class I discovered the agonies of love. Mr McCluskey was at the blackboard, writing out the measurements of several cubes, and we had to work out the various volumes in our copybooks. Anyway, as I was sorting out my books I noticed graffiti on my desk, in pink marker. It said: I LOVE JOHNNY COFFIN.

At first I hoped that maybe it was written by Julie Hegarty, but she wasn't even looking over at me. Then I started to become paranoid. Maybe Monkey Murphy wrote it to make me look stupid. In fact, *anybody* could have written it. The only thing for it was to blot it out. So I began to cover it over with black marker.

'Johnny Coughlan, what are you doing, boy?!' screamed Mr McCluskey. 'Why is that book standing up on your desk? What have you got there, boy?'

Mr McCluskey started to come towards me. If he saw the writing I knew he'd show me up. I had to think fast. So I thought: Yeah, I'll put something on the desk and he'll simply confiscate it. At least it'll be less embarrassing. I put my hand in my pocket to whip out some X-MEN NEW MUTANTS Collectors Cards. But my stupid hanky got in the way, and all I could do was pull it out. By the time Mr McCluskey reached me, this great big dirty hanky was on the desk, behind my maths book.

Mr McCluskey held it up by two corners, for all the class to see. It looked like a flag of crystallized bogeys.

'Johnny Coughlan, perhaps you can tell me why this is more interesting than finding the volume of a rectangular solid?'

Then Monkey Murphy said, 'Hey, sir, maybe he's one of those *snot vampires*.'

The whole class just burst out laughing. Even Julie Hegarty was laughing. Even my best friend Jimmy Pats Murphy was laughing.

'Well, Coughlan, as you are so interested in your handkerchief,' said Mr McCluskey, 'I want you to convert its *square* into a *cube*, and then work out its *volume*. Do it *now*, boy!'

So, in the history of the whole school, I'll be known as that kid who had to work out the volume of *a box of snots*.

an angel on Telly Bingo ...

In school on Friday I learnt all about the true function of literature. I didn't learn it from Mr McCluskey, and I didn't learn it from W B Yeats, and I didn't learn it from William Shakespeare, and I didn't learn it from that poet Milton. I learnt it from Julie Hegarty and Monkey Murphy. This is how it happened:

Mr McCluskey got some of us to read out the short stories we had written for homework. Julie Hegarty was the first, and so she began to read out her story, which was about an angel who kept appearing on somebody's television set. Nobody in the house could see the angel, except a little girl. Everyone in the family would be watching *Big City*, but all this little girl could see was the angel. And she'd say: 'Mam, what's that angel doing in *Big City*?' And her mam would say: 'There's no angel in *Big City*. What are you talking about?' And then everyone would be watching *Telly Bingo*, and the little girl would say: 'Mam, there's an angel on *Telly Bingo*.' And her mam would say: 'There's no angel on *Telly Bingo*. What are you talking about?' Everyone would be watching the news, and the little girl would say: 'Mam, there's an angel on the news.' And her mam would say: 'There's no angel on the news. Sure, that's only yer one reading the weather. What are you talking about?'

In the middle of the night the little girl got up and turned on the telly, and the angel came on the screen and started talking. The little girl's mother got up and found her watching the telly. But it was three o'clock in the morning and the telly was all fuzzy. 'What are you doing?' said her mother. And the little girl said: 'Mammy, look, there's an angel on the telly.' And her mother said: 'Sure, there's no angel on the telly, that's just a load of fuzz. Will you get back to bed.'

Now, by this point I was no longer listening. I was looking at Julie Hegarty's hair as she read out her story. The light from the classroom window was lighting it up like gold. When I came out of my trance I just caught the end of the story. In the end the television broke down and a man had to come and fix it. The man who came to fix the television said that it was completely burnt out and that they would have to get a new one. So they got a new telly, and the angel never came back again.

Julie sat down in her chair and the light from the window was shining all around her. Mr McCluskey told

Monkey Murphy to stand up and read *his* story.

At that moment the clouds must have come out, because the classroom suddenly got dark. Monkey's story was about a man who drank some water from a well, and as he drank the water a snake swam into his mouth and down into his stomach. But the man didn't know that the snake was in his stomach, and the snake grew and grew until eventually it ate the man from the inside out.

After thinking about these two stories I came to two conclusions. Number one: Monkey Murphy is definitely a psycho. Number two: Julie Hegarty is an angel.

When I got home I switched on the telly, but it wasn't receiving any signals from heaven. *Big City* was on, and there was no sign of Julie Hegarty.

i want you to work out the pi of infinity ...

Last night I dreamt that I was in school, and it was the start of class, and Mr McCluskey was calling me to the front of the classroom. When I got there I found myself standing in front of a small table, and on the table was this enormous snail. I mean *enormous*, like the size of a cabbage. And the snail had this weird pattern on its shell, like a black and white spiral.

'Now, Coughlan,' said Mr McCluskey, 'I want you to work out the pi of infinity.'

'What, sir?'

'*Infinity*, Coughlan, *infinity*. Heavens, boy, are you so stupid that you can't work out the pi of infinity?'

'But, sir, infinity goes on forever, and soon it'll be lunchtime. I won't even have time to finish the sum, sir.'

'Of course infinity goes on forever, Coughlan, that's why it's *called* infinity. And that's why we use *calculators*, Coughlan. Calculators were made so that we could work out infinity. So, use your calculator, Coughlan.'

I look down at the table at the ginormous snail. And it dawns on me that the snail is a calculator, because this is a dream, and in dreams *anything* makes sense. I pick up the snail and it begins to make a humming sound, so I pull one of its horns, and the spiral pattern on its shell starts to turn around and around, and as the spiral turns around the snail gets bigger each time, until the snail is as big as a television. And it's getting so heavy that I have to put it down, and the next thing this snail is beginning to fill up the room, and Mr McCluskey is shouting:

'Coughlan, boy, what have you done to the calculator?'

And I keep screaming, 'Please, sir, it wasn't me, sir, it was infinity, sir ...'

But the snail is so big now that the whole class is clinging to its shell and it's bursting through the ceiling, and the whole school is collapsing. There's tremors and earthquakes, and buildings are falling everywhere and the snail's just getting bigger and bigger, and Mr McCluskey is shouting: 'Coughlan, you've ruined infinity! You're a disgrace, boy, *a disgrace* ...'

just get a sword and make yourself useful ...

Mr McCluskey had told us that on Monday we would be performing *Romeo and Juliet* in class. I mean, we'd been studying this book for three weeks, and I hadn't even *read* it yet.

So, anyway, Mr McCluskey decided that Julie Hegarty was going to be Juliet, and Monkey Murphy had volunteered to be either Montague or Capulet, and preferably both. I had no idea who *these* two characters were, but made the logical assumption that they would probably get to *kill* somebody.

Then Mr McCluskey started to appoint people as Benvulio or Mercutio or Roly-Polio. I hadn't a clue who *they* were either. For all I knew, *Pinnochio* could have been in this play. The only question that remained was who was going to play Romeo?

Now, as Romeo was the lead part, and as he obviously had to be played by somebody of outstanding ability and good looks, it's quite obvious that *I* should have got to play him. Well, I didn't. I didn't get *any* part.

'Sir, is there anyone left, sir?'

'*Anyone left*, Coughlan?' growled Mr McCluskey. 'Yes, as a matter of fact, Coughlan, there is. *You*, boy, can be *William Shakespeare*.'

'But what does *he* do, sir?'

'Nothing, Coughlan, he just stood by and watched other people ruin his work.'

So there I was, standing on the sidelines doing nothing. You'd think Mr McCluskey would be happy. Far from it.

'You there, Coughlan, what the devil are you doing?'

'I'm doing nothing, sir. That's exactly what you told me to do. I'm just pretending to be William Shakespeare and I'm doing nothing.'

'Oh yes, Coughlan,' said Mr McCluskey sort of sarcastically, 'I just knew that a role that entailed doing absolutely nothing would suit you down to the ground. Well, Coughlan, I've changed my mind. You'd better be in the play after all. You can be an extra.'

'An extra *what*, sir?'

'An extra swordsman, Coughlan. You can play a guard or something. Just get yourself a sword and make yourself useful.'

So I had to stand around with a ruler, pretending it was a sword, and let me tell you, I looked like a complete wally. Of course, Monkey Murphy just loved it, because it meant that in the fight scenes he got to kill an extra person.

'*Mickey Murphy*, what the blazes are you doing, boy?'

'I'm killing Coughlan, sir. He won't die properly, sir.'

'*Coughlan*!' screamed Mr McCluskey, 'for heaven's sake, boy, will you die properly. You're holding up the entire play.'

So, in the interests of William Shakespeare I had to die about twenty times.

Yeah, English Literature, it's even worse than acne.

the Second Paradox of Zeno …

Mr McCluskey was standing in front of the blackboard with a brand new piece of chalk in his hand. He started to draw a circle, and around the circle he drew another circle, and then around that he drew another. And he just kept on drawing, circle after circle.

'*Johnny Coughlan*,' screamed Mr McCluskey, 'what

am I drawing on the blackboard, boy?'

'You're drawing circles, sir. Bigger and bigger circles, one outside the other.' It was *obviously* the right answer, because that's what he *was* doing. But as soon as I said it, I knew it *must* be wrong.

'No, *Coughlan*. I am not drawing circles *outside* circles, I'm drawing circles *inside* circles. The reason you think I'm drawing circles *outside* circles is because I'm drawing this *backwards*. What you see on the blackboard, class, is a *diagramatic representation* of the Second Paradox of Zeno. Now, can anybody tell me: what *is* the Second Paradox of Zeno?'

Orla Daly put up her hand: 'Is it a detergent, sir?'

'No, girl, it is not a detergent. The Second Paradox of Zeno states that eternity goes in both directions. Not only is it expanding outwards into space, and getting bigger and bigger, but it is also going the opposite way, and getting smaller and smaller.'

And do you know something? As I looked at the blackboard I knew that Mr McCluskey was right, and for the first time in my life I knew exactly what he was talking about. Because I could actually feel my brain, right inside my head, getting smaller and smaller and smaller. And all the maths and English Literature and history and geography and Irish that I ever learnt was disappearing into its rightful place: eternity.

Lara Croft was too old …

Today in school Mr McCluskey asked me two questions. One I got wrong and one I got right. But because I'm smarter than any teacher in the whole world, only *I know* which is which.

'*Johnny Coughlan*, perhaps you can come out of your coma long enough to tell me what I've just drawn on the blackboard?' screamed Mr McCluskey. Mr McCluskey is *always* screaming. I think it's something he picked up at Teacher Training College.

Anyway, even though I hadn't been listening to a single word Mr McCluskey had been saying all morning, it was *obvious* what was on the blackboard.

'Yes, sir. You've just drawn a picture of the Human Reproductive System, sir.'

'*What*, Coughlan? The *Human What*, Coughlan?'

Do you know, the way Mr McCluskey was carrying on, you'd think I'd got the answer *wrong*. And then, to confuse my brain even more, Julie Hegarty goes and

puts up her hand, as if there's a *better answer* than *mine*. And I'm thinking, *hang on*, this *is* a picture of the Human Reproductive System. Then she says, 'Sir, it's Argentina, sir.'

'*Yes, girl*,' said Mr McCluskey, obviously thinking that we were doing *Geography*, which is *after* the first break.

'*AR-GEN-TEE-NA*! Argentina, *Coughlan*, Argentina! It's Biology *after* the first break, you stupid boy! This is *Geography – Geography*!'

And it was exactly at that moment that I realised why being in love with Julie Hegarty was impossible. She was *always* going to have the right answer. But I wouldn't even know what the right *question* was!

At lunchtime, accepting that Julie Hegarty was beyond my reach, I went over my options. Lara Croft, the one with the tight T-shirt from *Tomb Raiders*, was too old. And anyway, she was far too busy killing zombies and doing adverts for fizzy drinks. That only left Misty, the one with the tight T-shirt from *Pokémon*. It was a tough one, but after lunch Mr McCluskey helped me make up my mind.

'*Johnny Coughlan*, if you can turn your mind away from *Biology*, boy, perhaps you could tell us *the exact function of fiction*?'

'Yes, sir,' I said, knowing the answer. 'The function of fiction is to create a small furry creature that will break your heart.'

Mr McCluskey held his breath. I could sense his brains moving about between his ears. He was *convinced* I was quoting someone like James Joyce, but he couldn't be sure. The thing is, I was quoting the creator of *Pokémon*, some Japanese guy whose name I couldn't pronounce even if my life depended on it. And the problem for Mr McCluskey was that he didn't dare contradict me, just in case I *was* quoting James Joyce.

That's the trouble with teachers. They'd be better off watching *cartoons*, and leaving *literature* to Shakespeare.

i want to go to prison ...

Oh yeah, that was it – we were in class doing an English exam. Anyway, I was chewing my pencil, hoping that I would get lead poisoning and be rushed immediately to hospital, when this shadow crossed over my desk. When I looked up I could see that Jimmy Pats Murphy was holding up a sheet of paper, and on it

was written: HEY, JOHNNY, WHAT PLAY DID PYTHAGORAS WRITE? Before I could whisper that I didn't care, Mr McCluskey was shouting at us to stop cheating.

Anyway, as a result, we spent the lunch break in detention, back in the same old corners. And that's when Jimmy Pats asked me this stupid question.

'Hey, Johnny, what's the most difficult game in the world?'

'Playing football with your right leg tied to your left ear.'

'No, I'm *serious*. Anyway, football's a *sport*. I'm talking about a *game*.'

'Okay, let's see. Chess.'

'No.'

'Chess played under six feet of water without oxygen?'

'No.'

'Chess played under six feet of water without oxygen and wearing a pair of wellington boots as gloves.'

'Nah, be *serious*!'

'Look, how can I be serious when I don't know the answer? Why don't you just tell me, you plonker.'

'Okay. The most difficult game in the world is the one they play in prisons.'

'Yeah, Jimmy. It's called *escaping*, and the reason it's difficult is because they can't do it.'

'Nah, I'm not talking about that. I'm talking about the game they play on their cell walls. You know the one ... it's a bit like noughts and crosses. But it's just all these lines, and they use a piece of chalk. And the rule is that they can only make one move every day.'

'You complete brain-space! That's not a game! They do that to mark off the days that are left till they get out of prison. That's why they only do *one mark a day*, you dork.'

'Nah, Johnny, that's what everybody *thinks* they're doing. But instead it's a secret game. I read about it on the internet. It said that the reason they only make one move a day is to save the chalk, because they only ever get one piece. This game is ancient, Johnny. They've even found the same markings in Egyptian pyramids, with a whole bunch of skeletons. And do you want to know the really scary part? No one's *ever* finished the game. *Ever*. And that's why some criminals keep going back to prison. Because they want to play the game.'

At that moment the bell rang for the end of lunch, so Jimmy Pats never finished what he was talking about. But do you know something, the more I think about it, the more it makes sense. And the more it makes sense, the more I want to go to prison.

as if it was a pair of mouldy underpants ...

Mr McCluskey was droning on about the allegorical fiction of Nathaniel Hawthorne, and, as usual, nobody was listening. You see, the thing with Mr McCluskey is that he's got this really cracked idea that we should be expanding our minds with all kinds of stuff from world literature. And because of this we end up doing things that no school in the *entire country* would do. Like, today we'd just read a chapter by this Hawthorne fella from *The Scarlet Letter*, and I didn't have a *clue* what it was about. I mean, this guy's sentences were so long that by the time you got to the end of one, you'd forgotten what the *beginning* was about.

Anyway, when Mr McCluskey turned around to write something on the blackboard, Jimmy Pats Murphy took it as the opportunity he had been waiting for to make a swap underneath the desk. So, I passed Jimmy Pats a copy of WAR HAMMER, and he passed me a copy of the OINK graphic novel. Unfortunately, Mr McCluskey happened to turn around just in time to catch us.

'*Johnny Coughlan*, what have you got there, boy?'

'Nothing, sir.'

'*Nothing*! *Nothing*! Nothing, Coughlan, is what you have between your ears, boy!'

Then, before I knew it, Mr McCluskey had snatched up the graphic novel and was holding it between his fingers as if it was a pair of mouldy underpants.

'*Coughlan*! This, *boy*, is a comic!'

I could see that Mr McCluskey's face was beginning to turn purple, which is always a very bad sign, and usually results in a dose of detention for the unfortunate victim. So I knew I'd have to think fast.

'Actually, sir, it's *a graphic novel*. It's a highly evolved form of literature that has influenced contemporary culture–'

'A *what* novel, Coughlan? This is a *comic*, boy, and it has no place in a classroom with Nathaniel Hawthorne.'

'But it does, sir. You see, it's *allegorical*, sir.'

'So it's *allegorical*, is it, Coughlan? Well, as you are obviously more qualified than I am, perhaps you could explain this *allegory* to the rest of the class.'

'Well, sir, you see, sir, it's called Oink because it's about this character called Oink, and he's half-pig and half-man. And it's set in the future, sir, in Australia. And there's been a nuclear war and everybody's running around demented because of the radiation. Anyway, this Oink wanders into the desert on his horse, which is just a horse, because the radiation didn't affect horses, and Oink's captured by these men who wear rubber suits. And anyway, they take him to the city, and all the people are starving. So then they take him to the sausage factory, on account of the fact that he's the biggest pig they ever saw in their lives, and then they try to turn him into sausages. But he's got these five guns, one called Monday, one called Tuesday, one called Wednesday, one called Thursday and one –'

'*Yes, yes, yes, Coughlan*,' screeched Mr McCluskey. 'But what's this got to do with *allegory*?'

'Well, you see, sir, it's like this: you can reduce the entire world to a state of anarchy, but people will still be eating sausages.'

Anyway, Mr McCluskey just didn't get it. But then, what would you expect from somebody who reads *Nathaniel Hawthorne*?

i knew she was TROUBLE ...

About half-way through the term this new girl, called Enya Murphy, joined the school. And let me tell you something, the very first moment that she came into our class I knew she was trouble. She had bright orange hair and sticky-out ears and was kind of cute, but when Monkey Murphy remarked out loud during break that her legs looked as if they were made of foam rubber, she just walked across the yard and punched him on the nose. Monkey fell to the ground and for a minute everybody thought he was dead. But actually, he'd only fainted. After that, everybody tried to steer clear of her.

If Enya asked you for a Tayto, you'd give her a Tayto. If she asked you for a sweet, you'd give her a sweet. If she asked you to do her homework, you'd do her homework. Within a week, everybody in the school had given up eating sweets and Taytos, and it wasn't even Lent. The only person in the entire school who

hadn't done any homework for her was me. But that's because I didn't even do *my own* homework.

Then, one awful day when the sky was black, Enya Murphy fell in love.

'Johnny, would you like a Tayto?' said Enya on that fateful day.

'No thank you, Enya, they only make me hyperactive.'

Enya looked at me with eyes the colour of lead. It was at that moment that I noticed her teeth for the first time. Every single one of them came to a point. As she continued to stare I decided that being hyperactive was probably better than being dead, so I said: 'Yeah, you know, Enya, I think I will have a Tayto after all.'

The following day Enya asked me if I'd done the essay on Gerard Manley Hopkins. We were supposed to have written two pages on this stupid poem he'd written about a pigeon or something. But the only conclusion I could come to after reading the poem, was that English was his second language. For a terrible moment I panicked, because I was convinced that she wanted to copy an essay that I hadn't even *done*. But she didn't want to *copy* my essay, she wanted to *do* my essay. I sat on the school steps, writing like mad, while she dictated the whole thing from memory. When she started saying that the poem was about a hawk, when it was quite obviously about a pigeon, I decided not to contradict her. It was just as well, because she was right.

By the end of the week Mr McCluskey was eyeing me with suspicion.

'Johnny *Coughlan*, have you recently been struck by lightning?'

'No, sir.'

'Well, that's very *odd*, Coughlan. Because your brain seems to have undergone an *inordinate* upsurge of activity.'

'It must be the Taytos, sir.'

'*Taytos*, Coughlan?'

'Yes, sir. They make me hyperactive.'

At night I began to have strange dreams about Enya Murphy. I dreamt that her teeth were becoming sharper and sharper, and that her legs were becoming longer and longer. I always woke up in a sweat. And every day she would give me Taytos and do my homework. Somehow, I suspected that it would all end in tears, but I didn't care. I had the best marks in the class, and I didn't even have to read any stupid poems about pigeons.

he'd just eaten the cat ...

As far as things go, Enya Murphy had had a pretty good day at school. True, Monkey Murphy had annoyed her by suggesting she dye her hair yellow to match her teeth, but she satisfied herself by dragging him to the school gate and tying his hair to the railings. In the end it took Mr McCluskey fifteen minutes to unknot Monkey's head, but Monkey refused to tell him what had happened, probably because being beaten by a girl was just *too embarrassing*.

Before the start of English, Mr McCluskey announced to the class that he didn't want this type of incident to occur again, as the school gate had just been painted. 'And while we're on the subject of school property, I want you to know that we *will* find out who removed all the classroom doors off their hinges. And if the culprit has any sense, he'll come forward of his *own free will*.'

The stupid thing was, Mr McCluskey was assuming that the culprit was a *he*. But the whole school knew who the culprit was, and it was a *she*. It was Enya.

'Enya, what the hell are you doing?' I said, as she unscrewed the door of the chemistry room.

'What does it look like I'm doing? I'm taking the door off. I need the screws from the hinges.'

'Uh, what for?'

'I'm making a cage for my pet crocodile, and my dad isn't home at the moment to give me any screws.'

'Hang on a second, are you seriously telling me that you've got a *pet crocodile*?'

'Yeah, but he's only small. Dad found him in our garden. He'd just eaten the cat, but Dad said I could keep him as long as he didn't eat my little brother. Anyway, you can see him for yourself tomorrow, after school.'

So after school Enya took me to her house. Her parents weren't home, so she took me straight out to the back yard. When we got there I saw this enormous wooden box, like some kind of mad wardrobe, except that it had all these wooden tunnels coming out of its side.

'Just stay here and don't move,' said Enya. 'I'm going into the cage to get the crocodile. I'll be out in a minute.'

When Enya was gone I considered running for my life, but I figured being eaten by a baby crocodile

couldn't be much worse than having my head tied to the school railings. Then I heard this little voice. 'Hey, mister, who are *you*?'

I turned around and saw that it was a little kid, obviously Enya's brother. He was the most disgusting-looking kid I'd seen in my entire life. Two big slugs of snot were dangling from his nose.

'I'm Johnny Coffin,' I said. 'Enya's just gone in to get her pet crocodile.'

The kid started to giggle like a leprechaun. 'Hey, mister, it's a really great crocodile. The udder day Dad brought it home and my mum was still asleep, and the crocodile went up the stairs and bited my mum and my mum flewed out the window and she landed in the dump, and den the crocodile broke my mum's ear and my dad fell and he landed in the bin.'

At that moment I could hear Enya coming through the wooden box, and whatever she had with her was making loads of noise. And it suddenly dawned on me that having your head tied to the school gate probably *wasn't* the worst thing in the world.

So I ran like hell ... and I didn't look back.

a waterfall was running down the stairs …

On Monday morning my girlfriend Enya was so pleased to see me after the weekend that she took my left ear and began folding it back over the top of my head.

'Agghhh, *you lunatic*, you're ripping my face off!'

'Yes, you rat. That's what you get for running off and leaving me on my own.'

'Look, Enya, just put my ear back where it belongs, and we can discuss this like normal human beings. I didn't mean to run off and leave you; it's just that I got *nervous*. I mean, it's not like you've got a pet *hamster* or something. Be reasonable, now, it's not every day that somebody's girlfriend introduces them to their pet *crocodile*.'

Enya let go of my ear, but she'd pulled it so much that it felt a bit loose.

'Okay, Johnny, I'll give you one last chance. But you

better not upset Gristle *this* time.'

'*Gristle*? Who the hell is Gristle?'

'That's what I call my crocodile, stupid. I call him *Gristle Bonehead*, because I think he should have a *proper* name. And after you ran away that time he got very upset, and sticky little tears began running down his face.'

'Ah, Enya, will you give me a break! Crocodiles only start to cry when they want to *eat* people. That's just *saliva* coming out of their eyes.'

Enya started to fold my ear back again, so I decided that it just wasn't worth arguing with her.

Anyway, by the time we got to Enya's house, things didn't look too good. Her parents were obviously still in the hospital, and Enya and her little brother were left on their own. I noticed that all the furniture was chewed to bits, and that the carpets were squishy with water. A waterfall was running down the stairs. Enya explained that the upstairs bath was overflowing.

'It's best to keep the house nice and wet, because Gristle likes it that way.'

At this stage I was beginning to get extremely nervous. 'Look, Enya, I'll just stand here on the living-room table while you get Gristle.'

'Don't be a wuss. Look, come into the kitchen and I'll show you the frog factory.'

'The *what* factory?'

'The *frog* factory. I'm breeding frogs in the kichen

sink so that I can feed them to Gristle. He's already eaten all the *dogs* in the street, and the only other thing he likes is raw sausages. But we can't keep buying sausages, it'll ruin us.'

When I got to the kitchen, Enya's little brother was making something out of plastic shopping bags on the kitchen table.

'What are you doing?' I said.

'I'm making parachutes for der frogs. I'm in charge of feeding der crocodile, and I'm gonna fro der frogs out der winda, and dey'll land near der crocodile's house. Dat way I won't have to go near him.'

Yeah, this was *definitely* a dysfunctional family. Then I looked out the window and saw this ginormous cat who only had one eye. The eye took up most of the room on his face, and he had this big red goldfish in his mouth.

'What the hell is *that*?'

'Oh, *that*?' said Enya. 'That's Cyclops, our cat. I mean, our *other* cat. Not the one that got killed by Gristle. And it looks like he's got the last of the Murphys' goldfish. He goes down to their pond every day and steals one.'

While she was talking, Enya was stirring some water in the sink. When I looked into it I could see that it was full of tiny frogs.

'They're much too small for Gristle now, but in two weeks time they'll be just the right size.'

'Yeah,' said Enya's brother, 'and by dat time I'll have made *hundreds* of parachutes.'

At that moment there was a tremendous racket from outside, and we could see that Gristle Bonehead was chasing Cyclops the cat. When Enya and her brother ran outside – not to *rescue* the cat, but to see it *get eaten*, I seized my chance. I scooped up all the frogs into a plastic bucket and took them down to the Murphys' pond, where I poured them all in. When I got back to the kitchen I remembered to pull the plug, so that Enya and her brother would think that the frogs had got sucked down the sink. I blamed it all on Enya, saying that it must have happened when she stirred the water.

They were both disappointed, because not only had they lost all their frogs, but Cyclops the cat had got eaten, in one crunching bite, by Gristle.

And as for Cyclops, by now he's *probably* in Heaven. Where, if there's any justice, fish will have wings and very sharp teeth.

what we need is a player who isn't concerned with football ...

'Johnny Coughlan,' screamed Mr McCluskey from the edge of the football pitch, 'have you screwed your body on *backwards* this morning, boy?'

We were just coming off the pitch at half-time and the school team was losing twenty-three nil.

'No, sir, the other team's just too good for us, sir.'

'Too *good*, boy!!? *Too good*! No, boy, they're not too good. You're just *too useless*, the lot of you. After half-time I want to see some goals, some *goals*!'

In the changing-room Jimmy Pats Murphy, our goalkeeper, just wanted to have a quiet nervous breakdown, but Monkey Murphy kept trying to strangle him.

'Get off me, you complete moron,' screamed Jimmy Pats. 'If you want to kill somebody, why don't you go and kill the other team? Anyway, you weren't so great yourself. What happened? Were your feet tied

together or something?'

'Listen,' I said, 'we've got to stop fighting. We're supposed to be having a rest!'

'Yeah,' said Monkey, 'well, the way *you* were playing, Coffin, you've already had *your* rest.'

'Yeah, yeah, yeah. Listen, rockbrains, it just so happens that all this arguing has given me an idea.'

'What are you talking about?' said Monkey.

'Well, our problem is, we were actually trying to play *football*. And that was our mistake. What we need is a player who isn't *concerned* with football. What we need is a player who's only concerned with *winning*.'

'Listen, snot-skin, we need a *whole team* like that.'

'Nah, you're not thinking. We only need *one player*. And I know the perfect person. *Enya Murphy*.'

'Ah, not that psychopath girlfriend of yours! Anyway, she's a girl! What does *she* know about football?'

'She doesn't *need* to know anything about football. She doesn't even have to *play* football. All she has to do is terrify the opposite team. *We'll* play the football.'

Anyway, we got word to Enya. Blister O'Flynn gave her his kit, and she took his place. When we came on to the pitch after half-time I could see Mr McCluskey looking at Enya. Next he looked at the sky. Then he looked at the ground. Then he looked at his watch. Then he looked back at Enya and a big grin came on his face, as if he'd just won the Lotto.

The first thing Enya did when she got the ball was to start running in the wrong direction. Then she gave the ball the mightiest kick you ever saw and sent it straight at the head of the ref. The ref froze in mid-air and fell down unconscious. The match was suspended for three minutes until he came to. By that time he was seeing double, and probably treble, and was so confused that he didn't seem to mind that Enya was running around the field like a mad cat, growling and spitting at every member of the opposite team. In the meantime, we got on with it, and played some football.

Now, we only managed to score seventeen goals, and we still lost the match. But Jimmy Pats Murphy, our goalie, had a quiet second half. And Mr McCluskey, who is usually very set in his ways, was brought round to the delights of *wimmin's football*.

turn yourself into a holy picture …

It was the lunch break and I knew that this time I'd be in for it.

'What's up with you?' asked my girlfriend, Enya Murphy.

'It's that stupid book we're supposed to have read for English. You know, *Beowulf*. Well, they should call it *bore*wulf. I just couldn't be bothered with it, but I know Mr McCluskey is gonna pick on me with the questions. I just know it. Why can't we be like every other school in the country and study something like Charles Dickens? Charles Dickens would be easy compared to *this* thing. I wish I could be like you. You seem to know all about this stuff.'

'Yeah, I know everything. But that's because I'm smart and don't bother to read the books. You can't learn anything from books, 'cos they were all written by idiots.'

'Ah, Enya, what the hell are you talking about? How can you know all about the books if you haven't read them?'

'Well, that's simple, Johnny. It's a thing I invented. It's called *creative literature*. First of all you look at the cover, and you remember what's on it. Then you read every three lines of the introduction at twenty-line intervals. Then you skim through the book and only read the parts where people look as if they're actually *doing* something. You know, like killing or being nasty. By then the whole thing will have come together in your head and you'll know what the book is about. But, of course, the best method of all is not to get asked any stupid questions in the first place.'

'Oh yeah, and how do I do that?'

'That's easy. I do it in every lesson. All you have to do is turn yourself into a holy picture.'

'Turn myself into a holy *what*?'

'A holy *picture*. You know, like one of those holy pictures where the eyes follow you about wherever you go, but you know all the time that the picture *can't really see you*, and it isn't really looking.'

So, during the rest of the break I followed Enya's instructions to the letter, and by the time I'd finished off the introduction and skimmed through the book I kind of knew what it was about.

'Johnny Coughlan,' screamed Mr McCluskey at the very start of the lesson, 'perhaps you could tell the class, as briefly as possible, the *entire plot* of *Beowulf*.' I looked around the class, and everybody looked like a holy picture. I mean, they were all looking at me, but I knew they were thinking about something else.

'Yeah, well, sir, it's basically a bit like the Mad Max Movies, except there aren't any cars. But you've got this guy called Beowulf, and he's a bit of a head-case, 'cos he likes killing things. And they're all in this hall having something to eat, and some guy makes a speech. Then this monster called Grendel comes to the hall and wrecks the place. Then Beowulf comes and makes a speech, they all have something to eat and he kills the monster. Then the monster's mother comes into the hall and wrecks the place, and some guy makes a speech, they all have something to eat, and Beowulf kills the monster's mother. Then they're in the hall again, this other guy makes a speech, and they have something to eat. Then this dragon comes along and kills Beowulf, but Beowulf kills the dragon at the same time. Then they have something to eat and this guy makes a speech.'

Anyway, before I'd even finished this litany of complete drivel, Mr McCluskey's eyes were rolling about inside his head. It was only when I stopped talking that Mr McCluskey's eyes came to a standstill.

'*This guy, that guy, and another guy*. Tell me, *Johnny Coughlan*, do you happen to *actually know* the names of *any* of the characters in this poem?'

What, was he kidding? I mean, these guys came from Denmark or Geatland or Jutland, or *some kind* of stupid place. Pronouncing their names would be like coughing with a sharp stone in your throat. So, for the first time that day, I told the truth.

'Actually, sir, I find their names totally unpronouncable, sir.'

'Coughlan ...'

'Yes, sir?'

'*Sit down,* Coughlan. And, Coughlan ...'

'Yes, sir?'

'*Stay down*, Coughlan.'

So I sat down and Mr McCluskey began looking at the class. Now, it was obvious to a teacher of Mr McCluskey's experience that the entire class was in a coma. He looked at Enya Murphy, then he looked at me, then he looked at Enya Murphy again. Enya was trying her best to look like a holy picture, but Mr McCluskey wasn't going to be fooled for one second. Not today, anyway.

'*Mizz Murphy* ... perhaps you could say something about the use of alliterative stresses in the poem, *Beowulf?*'

Enya's eyes unglazed. It was obvious that she knew she'd just been asked a question. But because, like, she'd been a million miles away, there was *no way* she could know what that question *actually was*.

Enya looked at Mr McCluskey with eyes the colour

of greasy washing-up water.

'Actually, sir, I simply refuse to comment on a poem which glorifies the killing of female monsters. Especially when they're *mothers*.'

Yeah, that's what I like about Enya: she's a real *intellectual*.

she'd been collecting this earwax for a month ...

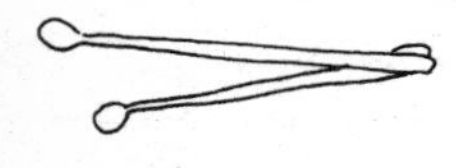

'Johnny Coughlan,' said Mr McCluskey during Religion, 'could you tell me what sixty and forty add up to?'

'Of course I can, sir,' I said, desperately trying to add sixty and forty. 'They add up to a hundred, sir.'

'*Wrong, Coughlan*. They add up to *one*.'

'One, sir?'

'Yes, Coughlan. *One*. And do you know why they add up to one, Coughlan? Of course you don't, boy, because you're only used to thinking in straight lines. And in your case, Coughlan, not *very long* straight lines.

In fact, very *short* straight lines.'

At this stage I started to look around the class, but I could see that nobody else had a *clue* what Mr McCluskey was talking about either. The only person who seemed to be in total control of the situation was my girlfriend Enya Murphy, who was rolling an enormous ball of earwax in the palm of her hand. She had got the earwax from her brother, who has probably the most disgusting ears in the entire country. Apparently she'd been collecting this earwax for a whole month, taking a little bit out of his ears each day. Why she actually *wanted* this earwax was a complete mystery, and I hadn't really the courage to ask her, but there she was, rolling it in the palm of her hand as if it was the most normal thing in the world.

'*Johnny Coughlan*, are you still paying *attention*, boy?'

'Yes, sir,' I said, totally forgetting what Mr McCluskey had been talking about.

'So, why does sixty and forty add up to *one*, Coughlan?'

'I don't know, sir.'

'Well, Coughlan, it is very simple. Because I am talking about *sixty pennies* and *forty pennies*, which as you know, add up to *one pound*. And the reason I asked you this question is to prove that the *greater number* can quite frequently add up to the *lesser number*. And do you have any idea what this has to do with *religion*, Coughlan?'

'No, sir.'

'Of course you don't, boy. Because if you did know I wouldn't have to be spending my time telling you. Well, Coughlan, there is no number greater than *one*, for it is the most complete number in existence, because all other numbers can be accommodated inside it. Therefore, Coughlan, it is the perfect symbol of infinity, because all other numbers, both the positive and the negative, can only exist if the number one *comes first*. ENYA MURPHY, WHAT THE DEVIL HAVE YOU GOT THERE, GIRL?'

'It's a ball of earwax, sir.'

'A ball of *what* wax?'

'Earwax, sir. And in case you're wondering why I have it in Religion class, it's a symbol of infinity, sir.'

'A symbol of *what*?'

'A symbol of infinity, sir. 'Cos it's small and round and sticky, just like infinity.'

The whole class looked at Enya Murphy. *Mr McCluskey* looked at Enya Murphy. *I* looked at Enya Murphy. In her hand she held the most *disgusting* ball of earwax you've ever seen in your entire life, and do you know something, not only did Mr McCluskey hesitate about confiscating it, but as she held it in her hand, we all believed that maybe it *was* the perfect symbol of infinity.

I mean, if infinity is *anything*, surely it's small and round and sticky?

the reason they call him Snots ...

'Hey, Johnny,' said Snots Murphy in the schoolyard. 'Do you want that chewin' gum?'

'*What*? Of course I want this chewin' gum. I mean, it's in my *mouth,* for crying out loud!'

'Nah,' said Snots. 'I mean, Johnny, do you want that chewin' gum when you've *finished* with it?'

'*What*? Snots, what the *hell* are you talking about?'

'I mean, *can I have it* when you've finished with it? I'm collecting used chewin' gums. I've already got a hundred and fifteen. Well, actually, only seventy-three of them are chewin' gums, the rest are bubble gums. And the bubble gums are the most interesting. 'Cos they've got different colours – I mean, used chewin' gums only come in grey or white. I've got some really interesting bubble gums. I've got a *black* one, which I found on holiday in Turkey. It was stuck to the bottom of my shoe. And I've got a pink bubble gum with six dead ants stuck to it. So, Johnny, can I have your

chewin' gum when you've finished with it?'

'Snots, you're *totally disgusting. Get the hell out of here*!'

I mean, did you ever hear anything so stupid in your whole life? My best friend Jimmy Pats Murphy, who's Snots Murphy's first cousin, tells me that Snots collects *bread wrappers*, and the tops off *disinfectant bottles*, and used *toothpaste tubes*, and he's even got a collection of those tiny stickers you get on *bananas*.

But the most bizarre collection he's got is the reason they call him Snots. Yeah, you guessed it – he even collects his own *bogeys*. He saves them up for a whole week and then sticks them to the underside of his desk. Tiny little blobs of bogeys. There's hundreds of them under there, like a load of stalactites. I mean, if they ever decide to clean the bottom of his desk, they'll have to use a *blowtorch* ...

trouble with my intestines ...

Being in love made writing essays very easy. Mainly because I didn't *have* to write them. My girlfriend Enya *wrote them for me*. Yeah, writing my essays was one of her most endearing features, and was far more preferable than having her fold back my ears or tie my hair to the school railings. But then, Enya's idea of affection isn't quite typical. Which is just as well. The time she kissed me she bit a hole in my lip, and I couldn't speak properly for a week. Speaking from personal experience, I wouldn't recommend having a psychopath as a girlfriend when you're only twelve years of age. But then again, if they're good at doing your homework, who cares?

Well, the problem is, Enya is *no longer doing* my homework. She hasn't been doing it for a week. And on the morning I'm telling you about, I couldn't finish my essay myself, which I was desperately trying to do during the morning break, because she dragged me

into the boys' toilets and stuck my head into the toilet bowl. 'That'll teach you to two-time me, you little rat.'

It wouldn't have been that bad really, except that Enya kept my head there until the cistern filled up again, so that she could flush it a second time. In the finish, she kept me there for the entire break, until I'd had the toilet flushed on my head about twenty times. This didn't make me exactly popular with those who were waiting to use the toilet, either. By the time the break was over, there was a queue of about twenty people, all bursting to go.

And the stupid thing was, I hadn't two-timed her at all. I'd simply told Julie Hegarty that I liked *her new shoes*. So here I was, sitting in class, soaked to the skin, with bits of toilet paper stuck to my head, and I knew that things could only get *worse*.

'*Johnny Coughlan*,' screamed Mr McCluskey from the front of the room, 'this history essay of yours is totally *incomprehensible*, boy!'

'Incomprehensible, sir?'

'Yes, Coughlan. *Incomprehensible*. Perhaps you could explain this sentence to me? *When the Egyptian kings died they had all their organs removed, including their Einsteins, which were rolled up and put into jars*.'

Personally, I couldn't see what needed explaining.

'I don't get it, sir? What do you mean, explain it to you? It means that when they died they had their Einsteins removed.'

‘Their *what*, Coughlan?’

‘Their Einsteins, sir. You know, that thing that helps you digest your food. It’s over thirty feet long and it sits beneath your stomach. *Come on*, sir, you *know this stuff*. It was *you* who told me in the first place, so it *has* to be true.’

Mr McCluskey glared at me as if I was a complete idiot. ‘*Coughlan*! Do you know what you are, boy? You are a complete *idiot*. It’s *intestines*, Coughlan. *Intestines*. Not *Einsteins*. Einstein was a *scientist*, not a length of gut in the human body. What’s wrong with you, boy? Are you *in love* or something?’

Everyone in the class turned and looked at me. Except for two people. Julie Hegarty and Enya Murphy. I suppose they didn’t look at me because they both thought they knew the answer. But one looked miserable and the other looked as if she owned the whole world.

Yeah, that’s the problem with love. It gets so bad that in the finish you don’t know your Einsteins from your intestines.

Monkey wouldn't be getting his pound ...

This morning I woke up and looked in the mirror and was greeted by a big green pimple on the edge of my chin. I mean, it looked like a watermelon. So, I did what most human beings do when confronted with a big green pimple on the end of their chins, I burst it. It always amazes me how much blood can come out of a tiny pimple, and before I knew it I had used half a toilet roll trying to stop the blood. By the time I looked in the mirror for the last time, I had a big red hole at the end of my face. I mean, is there actually a point to having pimples?

Anyway, on the school bus I tried to work out what I had in my favour and what I didn't have in my favour. On the minus side I owed Monkey Murphy a pound for lending me a pair of football shorts when mine went missing. The fact that Monkey had stolen my own shorts in the first place was irrelevant. The fact that the shorts he gave me were soaking wet and plastered in mud was also irrelevant. I still owed Monkey a pound. The fact that I didn't *have* a pound was *also* irrelevant, and I knew that Monkey would be waiting in the schoolyard for his money. Also on the minus side was the fact that I was three essays behind in my homework, and I couldn't even remember what the essays were supposed to be *about*.

To make things worse, my girlfriend Enya Murphy, who usually wrote my essays for me, was no longer talking to me. She wasn't talking to me because I had told Julie Hegarty that I liked her new shoes. Then I had told Julie Hegarty that her hair looked nice. Then I had asked Julie Hegarty would she come to the cinema on Saturday. I had done this on the grounds that Enya was no longer talking to me. Julie had said that she would think about it. Then Enya Murphy had given Julie Hegarty a black eye and thrown her new shoes on top of the roof of the girls' toilets. As a result *Julie Hegarty* was no longer talking to me.

I began to think about all the things I had that were on the plus side. But I couldn't think of *anything*. All I could think of was this enormous hole in the front of my face. Why does life have to be such a disaster when you're only twelve years of age?

Then I thought, *no, hang on a second*, you must have *something*. But all I had was a butterfly wing. It had been given to me by Enya Murphy and I had put it into my latest copy of JUDGE DREDD CLASSICS, as a bookmark. Enya had given it to me as a present because she said she loved me. She told me she had pulled the wing off the butterfly herself. It's the personal touch that counts.

When the schoolbus pulled into the yard I could see Monkey Murphy waiting for his pound. I could also see Enya. Her frizzy hair stood up on her head like an explosion of candyfloss. She had more spots on her face than the entire school put together, but she was the only girl in the world who had ever given me *anything*, even if it was a dead butterfly's wing. In that instant I knew what I had on the plus side.

So, when I got off the bus I told Enya that I was very sorry and that I still wanted to be her boyfriend. At that very moment Monkey Murphy asked for his pound, and Enya punched him on the nose. And now I had nothing left on the minus side. Because Enya would do my homework, Monkey wouldn't be getting his pound, and my girlfriend still loved me even though I had a big red hole on the end of my face.

One day somebody is going to solve the mysteries of love. But not yet.

the astrophysics of boils ...

Mr McCluskey had his back to the class and was writing multiplication sums on the blackboard. Actually, it was really quite ignorant of Mr McCluskey to think that he could teach us *anything* about multiplication, as it was a subject we knew all about anyway. I mean, for instance, most of us would go to bed with *one* spot. Probably on our noses or something. Then in the morning we'd have *two* spots. Then the next day we'd have four spots, then eight spots, then sixteen spots, then thirty-two spots. If only he bothered to look at our faces, he'd see that we were all walking *multiplication tables*.

'Johnny Coughlan! Are you daydreaming, boy?' screamed Mr McCluskey suddenly.

'No, sir. I was thinking about multiplication, sir.'

'Really, Coughlan! Then perhaps you could tell me what's eight times twelve?

'Yes, sir. It's ninety-six, sir.'

'Very good, Coughlan. There is obviously *some* activity left in your brain, after all.'

Yeah, well, he was wrong. All I did was look over at Monkey Murphy. The answer was written all over his face. That's the thing about spots. Everyone thinks they've got something to do with bacteria or hormones or something. But it's got nothing to do with hormones. It's all *maths*. One minute your spots are multiplying, then they're dividing, then sub-dividing. Then you've got all kinds of fractions, like cold-sores and whiteheads and blackheads. Not to mention the *astrophysics* of those enormous boils that you get at the back of your neck ...

'*Johnny Coughlan*! Are you daydreaming again, boy?' screamed Mr McCluskey once more.

'No, sir. I was thinking about fractions, sir.'

'*Fractions*, Coughlan! We're not *doing* fractions, Coughlan. *We're multiplying. Multiplying*!'

I looked at Mr McCluskey, and for the first time that morning I realised that he had a great big pimple growing on the side of his cheek.

Yeah, he was *right*. We were *all* multiplying.

'as you're a girl, I'll use my left hand,' said Monkey ...

Sometimes the hardest thing about a story is the beginning. That's because most stories have more than one beginning. And to make things worse, all the beginnings are happening at the same time. So, for instance, if I was to tell you this story, which I am, I'd have to either say, *Well, this all started with the clothes*, or *Well, this all started with the soap*. But it didn't. It started with *both*, at *the same time*. But as I've already told you that, I can start with *one at a time*. So ...

This all started with the clothes. But I won't start at the *beginning* of the clothes, I'll start at the *end*. Don't worry, it'll make sense when I've finished.

We'd been playing hurling, in the pouring rain, and I was soaked to the skin. But when we got back to the changing rooms I noticed that someone had stolen my trousers. 'I don't *believe* it! This is just *too much*. Haven't my trousers decided to go missing!'

'Ah, sure, Johnny,' said Jimmy Pats Murphy, 'how could your trousers decide anything? They don't have a brain. Besides, even your backside wasn't in them at the time.'

'Nah, you dork! I mean, *someone's taken* my trousers. First it was my socks. Then my underpants. Then my shirt. Then my jumper. Now my trousers.'

'I keep telling you, Johnny,' said Jimmy Pats, 'your clothes are the victims of *alien abductions*. Sure, haven't aliens been stealing clothes for *hundreds of years*. It's for all the bits of human DNA stuck to the dandruff and flaky skin and stuff. That's why *everybody* in the world is *missing socks*. The CIA proved it years ago.'

Yeah, well, trying to argue with Jimmy Pats Murphy's theories of aliens is like trying to *finish an essay on time*. A complete *waste*. So I didn't bother. I just went home wearing my soaking-wet football-shorts.

So, the next bit, which is actually the first bit, is the soap. 'Cos this all started with the soap. My girlfriend, Enya Murphy, for reasons known only to herself, decided to challenge the entire school to an arm-wrestling match. Yeah, that's right, the *whole school*. As a point of honour, and just to prove that he wasn't scared of her, Monkey Murphy decided to go first.

'As you're a girl, I'll use my *left* hand,' said Monkey.

After two seconds, Monkey's left hand was banged

against the desk. 'Okay, you've asked for it. I'll use my *right* hand.' After *one* second Monkey's right hand was banged against the desk.

'Right,' said Enya, 'as I won, you owe me. That'll be a bar of soap for each hand.'

'*What?*' said Monkey.

'I want you to give me a bar of soap for each time I beat you.'

'Yeah, sure, Enya,' said Monkey, 'didn't we all know you were desperate for a wash.'

Within *three* seconds, Monkey's *head* was banged against the desk. Anyway, Enya eventually took on the whole school at arm-wrestling, and each person she beat had to give her a bar of soap. And she beat *everyone*. So, by the end of the week, she had *dozens* of bars of soap. And the thing is, she *still* wasn't washing herself. I mean, you could *still* smell her before you saw her.

Everyone wondered what the *hell* she was doing with all the soap. So I asked her: 'Hey, Enya, what the *hell* are ya doing with all the soap?'

'Well, Johnny, come home with me after school and I'll show you. I've got it all in the garden shed.'

So after school I went home with Enya and we went inside her garden shed. And that's when the *two beginnings* of the story made *sense*. Inside the shed was all the soap. Enya had taken it all out of its packets and had made it wet, and then she'd squashed it all

together. She'd squashed it all together to make *statues*.

Statues made completely *out of soap*. A statue completely out of soap that looked exactly like her pet crocodile. A statue completely out of soap that looked exactly like her pet tortoise. Two statues completely out of soap that looked exactly like her two dead cats. And a statue completely out of soap that looked exactly like *me*. And guess *what*, the statue of me was even wearing my *clothes*!

'Hey, Enya, it's *you* who's been stealin' my clothes.'

'Yeah, Johnny. And aren't they just *lovely*.'

'Er ... Yeahhhh ... but, Enya ... what *is* this? It's an *art gallery*, right?'

I asked the question, but quite frankly, it looked more like a *zoo*.

'No, Johnny, you stupid dork. It's *voodoo*.'

'Er ... *what* doo?'

'Voodoo, Johnny, *voo-doo*? These are all the things I *love*. And they'll always be *mine*. 'Cos with these statues I can control my crocodile, my tortoise, my two dead cats, and my boyfriend. It's voodoo, Johnny, voodoo.'

So you see, it wasn't aliens from outer space. It was *voodoo*. Yeah, the *obvious* explanation is *always* the correct one.

half the class was coming down with brain-fatigue ...

I read this science fiction story once about this guy whose head was invaded by brain-worms. They're these worms that came from another dimension, and they started building their nests right inside his head. They ate his brain bit by bit and replaced it, bit by bit, with this big spongy thing. Anyway, this guy *didn't have a clue* that he had brain-worms, until one morning he wakes up and his head is twice the size it was before he went to bed. So he looks in the bathroom mirror but he can't remember who he is because he no longer has a brain. Well, that's not quite correct, because the brain-worms had taken over and now *they're* acting like his brain. *I am a brain-worm*, he says out loud. Then he goes down into the kitchen and gets himself a bowl of cornflakes.

Now, most so-called intelligent people, like parents and schoolteachers, just can't seem to get all this

science-fiction stuff. But, the point is, this guy was no longer in control of his own mind. And I know exactly how he felt, because I had a very similar experience. Except, my brain wasn't overtaken by brain-worms. *My* brain was invaded by *John Keats*.

Yeah, that's right, John *Pain-in-the-Brain* Keats. As usual, Mr McCluskey was droning on and on about this stupid poem that we were reading in English. I mean, even its title would give you *epilepsy*. It was called *La Belle Dame Sans Merci*, which is French for something, and it was the most *boring* thing I'd ever read in my entire life.

As I looked up I could see that *half the class* was coming down with brain-fatigue. Murphy-Murphy, as usual, was already fast asleep, but because he sleeps with his eyes open, Mr McCluskey didn't notice. But every now and then somebody's head would give a sudden jerk, and you could tell that they'd just caught themselves from nodding off. Jimmy Pats Murphy was so badly affected that he was trying to keep his two eyes open with his fingers. Everyone was squirming around in their seats, pinching themselves – *anything* to try to keep awake.

Anyway, the last thing I remembered was glancing over at Julie Hegarty. She was yawning like mad, and her mouth was opened so wide that I thought she'd swallow the classroom. Then, the next thing I know, she *is* swallowing the classroom. She's yawning and yawning and bits of the classroom are *vanishing*. First the blackboard, then the desks, then great big chunks of the walls. Then everybody in the class starts floating to the top of the ceiling. And there we all are, stuck to the top of the ceiling, *including Mr McCluskey*. But Mr McCluskey doesn't even seem to notice, and he's just droning on and on about John Keats and his stupid poem as if nothing has happened.

'What the hell is going on?' I hear myself saying out loud. Then I hear this dreamy voice. It's Murphy-Murphy.

'Hey, Johnny, relax. You're just dreaming. You're brain-rhythms have been taken over by John Keats's poem. It happens to *me* every English lesson. Welcome to the dream-time.'

'Hey, that's neat. You mean the whole class has fallen asleep, including Mr McCluskey?'

'Nah, Johnny, don't be stupid. The only people asleep are you and me. It's because we have highly developed brains, and have become psychologically transformed by the poem's alpha-rhythms. It's called *Negative Capability*. John Keats designed all his poems like this, so that they'd work on all those people with *sensitive minds*.'

I was just about to tell Murphy-Murphy that the reason we were asleep was because the poem was *incredibly boring*. But our conversation on the ceiling was suddenly interrupted.

'Coughlan, wake up, boy!' screamed Mr McCluskey, and I woke up with a start.

Everyone in the class was looking over at me. Everyone, that is, except Murphy-Murphy. He was still stuck to the ceiling. But nobody seemed to notice.

Mr McCluskey began to dance …

I was on the school bus with my girlfriend, Enya Murphy, when I suddenly noticed that she had a potato in her hand. It was a big knobbly-looking thing with clods of earth still stuck to it, and I saw that she was sticking bits of brown wool into the top of it.

'Hey, Enya, what the hell are you doing with that potato? I hope you're not doing any of that voodoo stuff again. I mean, you promised you wouldn't do any more voodoo stuff after Mrs Dooley's class thought they were a herd of goats and ran riot in the music room.'

'That wasn't voodoo. That was hypnotism. I promised I wouldn't do any more *hypnotism stuff*, I never said *anything* about not doing any voodoo stuff. Now, will you be quiet, Johnny. I'm trying to concentrate. You've got to concentrate when you're doing voodoo, otherwise it won't work.'

'Okay, but as long as you promise not to actually *kill* somebody.'

'Of course I'm not going to actually kill somebody. What would be the point of killing somebody? I mean, once they're dead you can't make them miserable anymore.'

At that point I thought it probably best not to say anything else, because trying to get through to Enya is like trying to communicate with another planet using bongos. But as she kept sticking those little bits of brown wool into the top of that potato my curiosity just got the better of me.

'Listen, Enya, what the hell are you doing?'

'Ah look, Johnny, if you don't stop annoying me I'll make a mistake. This is the tricky bit. I'm making a voodoo doll of Mr McCluskey and I'm doing the hair. If it doesn't look exactly like him then it won't work.'

So I watched Enya in silence for the rest of the journey. Through the windows of the school bus the sun shone off her orange hair, and her pimply skin looked like the surface of the moon. I was the only boy in the entire school who thought she was cute. Well, cute on the *outside*. On the *inside* she was full of ... *voodoo*.

In the classroom Mr McCluskey was having trouble concentrating. You could tell he thought it was the sun, which was casting its dusty beams onto the blackboard, but after he drew the blinds he *still* had trouble concentrating on the lesson. At first he seemed to have an intense *itch* on the back of his neck, which travelled, in about two minutes flat, down the centre of his spine. You could tell it had gone down his spine because he started poking down the inside of his jacket with a ruler.

Behind him on the blackboard were two words: Pádraic Pearse. But it didn't look like Mr McCluskey was going to get beyond those two words. By now the itch had travelled into his trousers. The whole class watched, mesmerised, as Mr McCluskey began to dance about the front of the classroom. Eventually, the lesson had to be cancelled, and we had a free period. Mrs Dooley had to sit in for Mr McCluskey, who had gone running down the hall like a lunatic, as if a rat or something had got stuck in his pants.

I looked over at Enya, who was still busy rubbing itching powder into the back of her potato. Up on the blackboard were those two words: Pádraic Pearse. Now, the only thing I knew about Pádraic Pearse was that he was shot by the British Army. But if Enya Murphy had been around with her potatoes, the course of Irish history would probably have been *very* different.

teachers do not like illogical behaviour ...

Enya Murphy had decided to organise the school's first annual snail race. The race was to be held in the boys' toilets during the last twenty minutes of the lunch break. The prize money, which Enya had generously donated from her own pocket, was ten pounds. The entry fee for the race itself, and I want you to pay special attention to this, because it's important, was the pair of shoelaces that you were wearing on your shoes. Enya was quite specific on this last point, and as a result everybody came to school that day with footwear that had laces. Monkey-boots, trainers, shoes, football boots, everyone, and I mean *everyone*, was wearing something that had laces.

Every single boy had been warned to use the loos well *before* the race, on account of the fact that they were gonna be filled with girls as well as boys. Enya had agreed to supply the snails, which she brought in a

large orange plastic bucket. Anyway, everyone got to pick their own snail, which wasn't very hard, as they all looked the same. There was only one exception to this, and that was *Enya's snail*. Enya's snail was the most insignificant little fart of a snail that you ever saw in your life. I mean, this thing was smaller than the nail on your little finger.

'Now,' said Enya, 'everyone has to write their own name on their snail. If a snail finishes the race without a name on it, it'll be disqualified.'

'Hey, Coughlan,' sneered Monkey Murphy, 'I don't care *who* wins this stupid race. 'Cos the odds are that your psycho girlfriend will have to give her ten pounds to *somebody*.'

Anyway, the snails were lined up at the chalk mark, and off they went. Anyone who's been to a snail race, and this was my tenth, will know that snails move *fast*. They only move slowly in *gardens*, where they've got no incentive to go anywhere. But in *toilets*, which isn't their natural habitat, they just want to get the hell out of there. Within two minutes there were snails *everywhere*. Snails going backwards, snails going sideways, snails in the urinals, snails in the toilet bowls, snails up the walls, even snails on snails. All, that is, except Enya's tiny little snail, which seemed incapable of travelling in anything *but a straight line*.

The entire school watched, crammed inside the boys' toilets and nearly passing out from the smell of stale wee, as Enya's snail won the race as if born to it.

Everyone left the boys' toilets feeling dejected, except for Enya, who now had a plastic orange bucket full of shoe-laces. Out in the yard chaos soon appeared in the form of the entire school trying to walk in shoes that flapped about for want of laces. Slap slap slap went hundreds of shoes at once, and when Mr McCluskey came to call us into the school he just stood with his mouth open.

As his entire class marched into the room in front of him he said nothing, but he eyed us all with nervous suspicion. Teachers do not like illogical behaviour. It just freaks them out.

We sat at our desks, and as Mr McCluskey entered the room he slammed the door behind him, as was his usual habit. It was at that moment that the most complex pulley-system of shoelaces known to the mind of man revealed itself for all to see. Triggered by the slammed door, the plastic orange bucket, full to the brim with water, travelled the entire room on a ribbon of shoe-laces, and deposited itself over the entirety of Mr McCluskey's head.

Well, you don't have to be a genius to guess that we were all kept in for an hour's detention. Everyone, that is, *except* Enya Murphy. Mr McCluskey had no doubts in his mind whatsoever that she was innocent of the whole ridiculous enterprise. For she was the only one in the entire class who still had laces in her shoes.

it's French for Kit-Kat ...

Because of the nasty trick that Monkey Murphy had played on my best friend, Jimmy Pats Murphy, Jimmy Pats had sworn he'd get his revenge. Personally, I thought that as far as nasty tricks go Monkey Murphy deserved ten out of ten. Yeah, in the Guinness Book of Nasty Tricks, it was in a league of its own. But then again, getting revenge on Monkey Murphy is as good as it gets. But wait a minute, let's go back to the beginning, otherwise this won't make any sense.

On Monday, Monkey had informed Jimmy Pats Murphy that he needn't worry.

'Hey, Jimmy Pats, you needn't worry,' said Monkey. 'You needn't worry about it one bit.'

'Worry about what?' asked Jimmy Pats, suddenly worried.

'Worry about doing your history essay, blockhead. 'Cos you see, I'm gonna do your history essay for you.'

Now, being a reasonably intelligent person, Jimmy

Pats immediately smelled a rat. A really *dead* rat. 'Nah, Monkey, it's okay. I can do my *own* essay. But thanks anyway.'

'Well, that's where you're wrong, Mister Brainache. You can't do your own essay, 'cos you're gonna be too busy doing *my* essay.'

Yeah, for a nasty trick, it was a pretty good one. 'But don't worry, Jimmy Pats. Mr McCluskey will never know I did your essay for you, 'cos I'm gonna disguise my handwriting.'

So Monkey Murphy did Jimmy Pats's essay with his *left hand*, and Jimmy Pats did Monkey's essay with his *right hand*. And Monkey's essay, which Jimmy Pats had done, got a B-Plus. But Jimmy Pats's essay, which Monkey had done, got an F. Yeah, that's an F as in *eff*. On top of that, Mr McCluskey got Jimmy Pats to write the essay out again, because he couldn't read the handwriting. And because the essay he did the second time was the same as he did the first time, which Mr McCluskey thought had been written by *Monkey*, Jimmy Pats got detention for *copying* off of Monkey.

I'm telling you: worthy of the Guinness Book of Nasty Tricks. But then, on Friday, Jimmy Pats had his revenge.

We were in the school bus, on the way to the swimming pool, and I was counting how many imaginary Monkey Murphys the school bus was running over. But then I lost count, because the *real*

Monkey Murphy came over to our seat.

'Hey, Mister Brainache, are you gonna eat that chocolate or what?' said Monkey. Jimmy Pats was holding a bar of chocolate in his hand. He'd been holding it for most of the journey.

'Monkey, will you give me a break! I'm *thinking* about eating it,' said Jimmy Pats. 'Now, will you get lost. You're breaking my *concentration*.'

'Look, Brainwave,' said Monkey, 'let me give you a lesson in *eating* chocolate,' and Monkey just snatched the bar from Jimmy Pats' hand. Monkey looked at the wrapper, but then he got confused. 'Hey, Mastermind, what kind of stupid chocolate is this, anyway? It says *Kak-Kak*.'

'That's 'cos it's French chocolate,' said Jimmy Pats. 'My aunty Eileen brought it back from Paris. It's called *Kak-a-Lak*. It's French for Kit-Kat.'

So Monkey went off with his bar of Kak-a-Lak, and ate the lot.

On the way off the school bus, I picked up the discarded wrapper, and read the writing. I thought it would improve my French, but it turned out to be written in English. It said: *Kak-a-Lak, Chocolate Laxative, the pleasant way to beat constipation. Do not exceed one square per day*. Doing some quick sums, I figured that Monkey had eaten about *twenty squares*. And all in three minutes.

In the changing rooms, Monkey decided to flick

everybody's body with a dry towel. Listen, when you're changing out of your underpants and into your swimming togs, getting flicked with a dry towel is as bad as getting flicked with a wet one.

Anyway, by the time we got into the pool, Jimmy Pats Murphy had turned to the subject of swimming-pool security: 'Hey, Johnny, don't forget, now. Don't go for a wee in the pool, 'cos they got this new detection system. You see, they've invented this dye, and when you pee in the pool it turns blue and points these great big arrows at you.'

Personally, I didn't quite get what Jimmy Pats was driving at. But then, after about five minutes, I understood completely. He was trying to give me a coded message. Because that's when this enormous pooh – and when I say *enormous*, I mean the size of *Manhattan* – came floating down the pool. Man, you should have seen it! Everybody got out of the water as fast *as a fart.* Everybody *except* Monkey Murphy. You see, he hadn't quite *finished* ...

Yeah, Monkey Murphy. On Monday he got into the Guinness Book of Nasty Tricks with a *nasty trick*, and on Friday he got into the Guinness Book of *Records* with the biggest turd in the whole world. You just had to admire his style.

yeah, a budgie ...

Mr McCluskey was standing in front of the blackboard with his back to the class. He was writing something up on the board, but we couldn't see what it was because he was in the way. The sun was shining through the windows and everything was normal. Gravity was still working, the sky was still blue, and bananas were still my favourite fruit. But just in that second something happened and suddenly things weren't so normal anymore. Don't get me wrong, gravity was still working, the sky was still blue, and bananas were still my favourite fruit, it was just that, well, I suddenly noticed that Mr McCluskey had a great big hole in the back of his trousers.

'Sir!'

'Be *quiet,* Coughlan,' growled Mr McCluskey, without even turning around. 'I'm trying to write something on the board, boy. You can ask your question when I'm finished.'

'But, sir, you've got a hole in your trousers, sir.'

At this the whole class burst out laughing, and Mr McCluskey turned around.

'*What*, Coughlan? I've got a *what*, Coughlan?'

'A hole in your trousers, sir.'

And that's when Mr McCluskey saw the second thing. In fact, that's when the whole class saw the second thing. The second thing was a budgie. Yeah, a budgie. It was flying around the classroom, very high, right up close to the ceiling. We all looked up and watched it, going around and around. Then, after going around about five times, it flew straight over to Mr McCluskey and landed on his head. Mr McCluskey just stood there, not quite knowing what you do when a budgie lands on your head, when the budgie suddenly let go of a big milky dollop of budgie droppings. As the budgie flew off, and out through the window, the droppings slid over Mr McCluskey's forehead and fell to his nose. Gravity, obviously, was still working.

After lunch, Mr McCluskey came to the class with a change of trousers. Well, they weren't trousers exactly, because he didn't have time to go home, so he had to borrow a pair of overalls from the caretaker. On top of that, his hair was still wet, because he had to wash out all of the bird droppings.

However, half-way through the lesson there was a flutter at the window and the budgie returned. It flew five times around the ceiling and then landed straight back on top of Mr McCluskey's head. Mr McCluskey tried his best to look dignified, but the budgie let go a second dollop of bird-droppings and flew off through the window. As the budgie disappeared into the distance I looked at the sky. It was still blue.

After the afternoon break Mr McCluskey returned to class with his hair even wetter than before. Anyway, no sooner had the lesson started than there was this fluttering at the window and the budgie flew in again. This time, though, Mr McCluskey wasn't gonna have any budgie fertilize his head, so he chased it around the classroom about six times until it flew out through the window. Then, just to be safe, I dropped my pencil. But it was okay, because gravity was still working and the sky was still blue.

After school I noticed that my girlfriend Enya Murphy was hanging around the schoolyard.

'Hey, Enya, are you coming home or what?'

'In a minute, Johnny. I'm waiting for Fred.'

'Fred? Who the hell is Fred?'

'He's my pet budgie. I've trained him to enter buildings, fly round the room five times, then crap on the head of the tallest person there. I got him as a birthday present from my Aunty Bridie. I feed him on raisins and live beetles, and he's a great comfort in times of loneliness.'

As I looked at Enya's spotty face and bright orange

hair, I was reminded of another reason why I was in love with her. It wasn't her good looks. It was her sense of gravity.

I opened my school bag and took out a banana. They were still my favourite fruit.

'he's not a cat, dear. He's a Buddhist ...'

Everyone in the world has someone in their family who's religious. I mean, *everyone*. It doesn't matter *what* kind of a person you are. Think of anyone you like, and there's someone in their family who's into religion big time. Even the Pope! Although, in the Pope's case, it's probably himself. Anyway, in my family it's my aunty Betty.

But before you go jumping to any conclusions as to what kind of a person my aunty Betty is, I better explain something. When I say that she's into religion, I don't mean she's narrow-minded or anything like that. In fact, she's so open to other ideas that her cat is a Buddhist. Yeah, that's right, a Buddhist.

So you're probably thinking, yeah, but what if her cat dies, and her new one gets a different religion? Well, the thing is, this cat *has* died. I mean, this cat dies about three times a year. He gets run over, eaten by dogs, electrocuted, drowned, strangled ... you name it, he gets dead. He's been struck by lightning, struck by cars, struck by hailstones the size of cabbages, and just about anything else you could mention. He's about the unluckiest cat you ever met in your life. Like, forget about nine lives, this cat has had about *sixty*.

'Hey, Betty, I see you've got a new cat,' Dad will say.

'No, dear, it's the same cat I've always had.'

'But, Betty, this cat's got ginger stripes,' Dad will say. 'Your last cat was black.'

'No, dear, it's the same cat I've always had. He just got killed and he's been reincarnated. He's a Buddhist, dear. You can't kill Buddhists, they just go on for ever. The only thing is, they always come back as cats or dogs. That's why I'm a Catholic, dear. I couldn't be bothered coming back as a cat. I mean, they're quite disgusting creatures really.'

'Listen, Betty,' Dad will say, 'if you think cats are so disgusting, how come you've got one as a pet?'

'He's not a cat, dear. He's a Buddhist.'

Yeah, that's the trouble with Dad, he just doesn't understand *anything*.

Mind you, at face value this religion thing can be

pretty confusing. But once you get the hang of it, it can be quite rewarding. I mean, I'll give you an example. Okay, let's see ... for instance, there's those miraculous medals. My girlfriend Enya wears them all the time. She's never seen without a miraculous medal.

'Hey, Enya, what's with the miraculous medals?' I said to her once.

'Oh Johnny, I'm never without a miraculous medal. They're fierce handy. I mean, if you need a screwdriver, they'll turn any kinda screw you could mention. Who needs to carry around a screwdriver when you've got a miraculous medal?'

And then there's those holy statues. For my eleventh birthday my aunty Betty gave me a plaster statue of the Child of Prague. And for Easter I got a plaster statue of Padre Pio. For Christmas I got a plaster statue of Saint Joseph, and on Saint Patrick's Day I got a plaster statue of Saint Patrick. And the thing about these plaster statues is that they always came with their heads broken off. I don't mean that their heads were missing, it was just that every single one of them came with their heads stuck back on with sellotape. At first I thought that maybe they'd been broken by aunty Betty's cat. But the mystery was solved by Jimmy Pats Murphy, who knows all kinds of stuff, even religion.

'Hey, Johnny, I see you've got a fine collection of holy statues,' said Jimmy Pats.

'Yeah, yeah, they're great. I'd sell them to a collector, only they've all got broken heads.'

'Do you know, Johnny, you're just *thick*. Don't you know *anything* about religion? Don't you know that it's fierce lucky to break off the head of a holy statue before you give it to somebody. That's why whoever gave you these statues, broke off their heads first. It's to bring you luck. I bet you don't even know about *the money*?'

'Jimmy Pats, what the *hell* are you talking about? What money?'

'Ah, Johnny, you're such a dork! The money they put inside the statues after they've broken the heads.'

'Do you know something, Jimmy Pats, I think *you're* the one who's broken his head.'

'Nah, Johnny,' said Jimmy Pats. 'Look, I'll prove it to you.'

Then Jimmy Pats broke open a statue and inside was *a fiver*. Within a minute we had every single statue broken into bits. But I don't think it was actually *vandalism*, because we made twenty quid, so it must have been *economics*. And don't worry about the statues. They hadn't got broken. They'd just got *reincarnated*. Into money.

Yeah, that's right, they must have been *Buddhists*.

she was painting her pet crocodile …

On Monday morning I called on Enya on the way to school. She'd phoned me the evening before and told me to turn up early. Now, what she needed me for I had no idea, but when I arrived at the front door I was greeted by her little brother. He was in the middle of having a wash, and the facecloth was still in his hand. Well, I assumed it was a facecloth, because he was rubbing it all over his nose, but quite frankly, it looked more like a dishcloth.

'Hey, it's about time you gave that facecloth a wash,' I said, 'it looks disgusting.'

'It's not a flaceclot,' said Enya's brother, 'it's a dishclot. Enya won't let me use der flaceclots 'cos she says I cover dem in snots. So I use der dishclots instead.'

Grateful for this information, I made a mental note not to eat out of any of the dishes in Enya's house ever again.

'Enya's in der kitchen, but ya better bring yer schoolbag with ya, 'cos she wants ya to carry der sausages.'

Now, I didn't have a *clue* what he was talking about, but by the time I got to the kitchen I was even more confused. On top of the kitchen table were about fifty packets of sausages. Enya was kneeling on the floor with a can of spray-paint in her hand and she was painting her pet crocodile. The crocodile was staying perfectly still while she covered his body in gungy brown paint. I noticed that the crocodile didn't have a lead on or anything, so I decided it would be safer if I didn't stand on the kitchen floor. I climbed up onto the kitchen table.

'Enya, what the hell are you doing? I mean, you're painting your crocodile *brown*. But you're crocodile's *already* brown.'

'Nah, Johnny,' said Enya, 'Gristle is *dark brown*. I'm painting him *beige*. You just have no sense of colour.'

'Ah, for cryin' out loud, Enya, whoever heard of painting a crocodile? Why don't you just leave him the way he is?'

'Do you know something, Johnny, you're such a dork! I'm not *painting him*, I'm *camouflaging him*. I'm changing his colour to beige so that he matches the floors and walls of the classroom. That way Mr McCluskey won't notice him when I bring him into school.'

'*What*! Enya, are you off your head, or what? You can't take your crocodile to school. I mean, he'll probably end up eating somebody. It'd cause a scandal. We'd all get detention. Like, *for life*!'

'Ah Johnny, will you stop being such a wuss. He isn't gonna eat anybody. That's why we're bringing all those sausages. As long as we feed him sausages all day long, he'll be as quiet as a mouse. So, shut up, will you, and start packing the sausages into your schoolbag. I have to bring Gristle to school for the whole week, because my mam and dad are coming back from the hospital on Friday, and my aunty Bridie is bringing in the builders to fix the house after we wrecked it.'

Anyway, about half an hour later Enya had finished painting her crocodile, so we left for school. In the back garden she pulled down the washing line, which I noticed she had already painted beige, and she tied it around Gristle's neck. When we got on the school bus the driver didn't notice that we had a crocodile with us, because it was so low on the ground, but he spent the entire journey screaming to the passengers to get down from their seats.

It was the same thing at the start of class.

Mr McCluskey came into the room and everyone was standing on their chairs, except for Monkey Murphy, who was standing on his desk. Oh, and of course, Enya, who was sitting down and sorting out the piles of sausages.

'*Sit down*, class,' growled Mr McCluskey.

'Good morning, sir,' we all said.

Mr McCluskey looked at us as if we were *deaf* or something, then he started *screaming* at us as if we *were deaf* or something:

'*Sit down*, class.'

Everybody stayed standing on their chairs, except, as I said before, Monkey Murphy, who was standing on his desk, and Enya Murphy who was sitting down counting packets of sausages. And I thought to myself, *Okay, this is it, Enya's done it this time; Mr McCluskey will blow his top and then somebody's gonna tell him there's a crocodile in the room*. But then Mr McCluskey's attention was suddenly attracted elsewhere.

'*Enya Murphy*, what the *blazes* have you got on your desk, girl?'

'They're sausages, sir. They're for my domestic-science project, sir.'

'Well, put them away, girl. In all my years of teaching I haven't come across a single class as *deranged* as *this one*.'

At that very moment the whole class held its breath, because Enya's crocodile was waddling its way towards Mr McCluskey's table. *Oh man,* I thought, *the crocodile's gonna eat Mr McCluskey and we'll get detention for a year*. And all the while, Mr McCluskey was screaming at us to get down and sit on our chairs.

But then the *weirdest* thing happened. When the crocodile got to Mr McCluskey's table, it just stayed right underneath it, as still as could be. So we all sat down on our chairs. Mr McCluskey sat down as well, obviously satisfied that we had finally decided to obey him.

Enya's crocodile stayed there all day long, inches away from Mr McCluskey's feet. But anytime Mr McCluskey got up to write on the blackboard, Enya would throw a bunch of sausages which the crocodile would snap up into its mouth. After a while the class began to relax. It was as if having a crocodile in the room was the most normal thing in the world.

After all, as bad as crocodiles are, they can't give you *homework*.

'Johnny, it's a conspiracy ...'

On Thursday morning the entire class boarded the bus to take us on the school outing. We were supposed to be going to the local cornflakes factory because Mr McCluskey was of the opinion that it would be educational. I mean, will you give me a break! How could anyone imagine that cornflakes could be educational? I mean, they're not even interesting. Yeah, that's right, 'cos cornflakes must be the most *boring* breakfast on the face of the earth.

Anyway, it looked as if I was the only one in the school who thought this was gonna be a wasted day. Jimmy Pats Murphy was sitting in his seat blathering on about how cornflakes were the secret weapons of an alien civilisation.

'You see, Johnny,' said Jimmy Pats, 'cornflakes are the perfect way to control the world, because everybody eats them.'

'Jimmy Pats, what the hell are you talking about, you complete *brainache*? How can cornflakes control the world?'

'Well, Johnny, it's a well-known fact that cornflakes were invented by aliens. The CIA proved it years ago.'

'Ah, will you get real! Cornflakes were invented in America by two brothers. And I know that for a fact 'cos I read it on the back of a box of cornflakes.'

'Of course you did,' said Jimmy Pats, 'and who do you think puts all that writing on the boxes? It's the aliens, you dummy. They're brainwashing you. They're brainwashing the entire planet, so that everyone will eat cornflakes.'

'Okay, Okay ... look, let's just suppose for one

minute that cornflakes *are* made by aliens. So what? What harm can cornflakes do?'

'Well, Johnny,' said Jimmy Pats, 'that's the brilliant thing about it. You see, it's all the extra iron and vitamins that they put into the cornflakes that does the damage. There's so much iron in an average bowl of cornflakes that it interferes with your *magnetic field*. And all these aliens are tracking our magnetic fields from *outer space*, on account of all the cornflakes we eat. I'm telling you, Johnny, it's a conspiracy.'

Man, that Jimmy Pats Murphy. One day his brain is gonna be probed for intelligent life. Anyway, I couldn't listen to this rubbish any longer so I turned around and tried to talk my girlfriend, Enya. But Enya wasn't interested in talking because she was reading this dumb book by someone named Sigmund Freud called *The Interpretation of Dreams*.

'Hey,' said Jimmy Pats, 'what's Enya reading?'

'Some stupid book called *The Interpretation of Dreams*,' I said.

'Hey, Johnny,' says Jimmy Pats, 'that's a really cool book. I've read it myself, about fifteen times. It's written by the guy who invented the vacuum cleaner.'

'Ah, for crying out loud, Jimmy Pats, will you get real! The vacuum cleaner was invented by a guy called Hoover. That's why they call them *hoovers*, you dork. *The Interpretation of Dreams* was written by Sigmund Freud. It says so on the cover of the book.'

'Well, Johnny,' said Jimmy Pats, 'that's where you're wrong. Sigmund Freud and Hoover invented the vacuum cleaner *together*. They were cousins. They also invented the Psycho-ceramic Ear.'

'What the hell are you talking about? I've never even *heard* of the Psycho-ceramic Ear.'

'Well, Johnny, that's 'cos it never caught on. People preferred vacuum cleaners.'

Man, I thought, *talking to this guy is just a complete waste of time*. Anyway, the bus was pulling into the factory gates so we started to get off. As Monkey Murphy was getting off the bus, I noticed that he was carrying a large plastic sandwich box.

'Hey, Monkey,' I said, 'you're not supposed to take your lunch into the factory. We're gonna eat our lunch afterwards on the bus.'

'It ain't my lunch, you dork,' said Monkey, and he opened the plastic box so I could see inside.

'Ah Monkey, that's *disgusting*! What the hell have you got in there? It looks like chopped-up insects or something.'

'Yeah, well, the reason it looks like chopped-up insects is because that's exactly what it is, you idiot. I spent all of yesterday collecting them. I've got bits of spiders and grasshoppers and flies and moths, and when I get into that stupid factory I'm gonna mix them in with the cornflakes, so that some morning some stupid moron is gonna end up eating them by mistake.

What do you think? Pretty cool trick, isn't it?'

Anyway, just as Monkey was finished talking, Mr McCluskey came off the bus and started counting the class.

'*Mickey Murphy*, what the devil have you got there, boy?' screamed Mr McCluskey, when he saw the plastic sandwich box in Monkey's hand.

'Please, Mr McCluskey, it's my lunch, sir,' said Monkey, lying through his teeth.

'What have you got your *lunch* for, boy? It's only ten o'clock,' screamed Mr McCluskey, his face going purple.

'Sorry, sir, but I was hungry, sir. I didn't have any breakfast,' said Monkey.

Mr McCluskey eyed the sandwich box with suspicion.

'Well, if you're that hungry, boy,' said Mr McCluskey, 'you'd better eat your lunch *now*.'

So Monkey had no choice but to have a go at eating his box of insect bits, while we all watched.

After our tour of the factory, we all got to take home a free box of cornflakes. Except, of course, Monkey Murphy, who wasn't hungry any more. Yeah, visiting the cornflakes factory was pretty educational, after all. Even if we didn't actually get to see any aliens.

Padre Pio, he's your man ...

Jimmy Pats Murphy had entered the all-Ireland Junior Monopoly championships, and had got through to the semi-finals. So that's when he decided to have a practice match.

'Look, Johnny, come round to my house on Saturday, and bring as many people as you can, even that psycho girlfriend of yours. And I bet I'll thrash the lot of you.'

When I mentioned the game of Monopoly to Enya she wasn't impressed.

'What would I want to play Monopoly for? Monopoly's for wusses. Why doesn't Jimmy Pats take up boxing or karate or black magic or something? I mean, *Monopoly*! Anyway, on Saturday I want to sort out my collection of carving knives.'

'Ah, come on, Enya, Jimmy Pats thinks this is really important. He's my best friend, even if he is a complete nutter, and I can't let him down.'

Anyway, Enya eventually came around to the idea and decided she'd give it a go. So on Saturday I went to her house to collect her. She was waiting for me in the front garden, sitting on the wall. Her frizzy orange hair was tied up at the front in two mad pigtails that stuck out like horns. She was wearing a pair of biker boots, black leather trousers and a Padre Pio T-shirt.

'Hey, Enya, what's with the T-shirt? I thought you were into Dr. Death and the Beastie Boys.'

'I am, Johnny,' said Enya, 'but I have a great devotion to Padre Pio. He could do some really neat things, like walk through walls and read people's minds. And he had this really great trick where he'd bleed all over the floor and he wouldn't even need a blood transfusion. And he could appear in two places at once and only needed a haircut twice, once in 1933 and again in 1956.'

'Hey, he sounds cool. Like one of the X-Men.'

'Yeah, you got a much better quality of saint during the first half of the twentieth century. Not like the plonkers you get these days.'

When we got to Jimmy Pats Murphy's house there was a whole crowd of people there. Julie Hegarty was there, and Snots Murphy, and Orla Daly, and Monkey Murphy, and Blister O'Flynn. Jimmy Pats opened the door.

'Hey, Enya, I like the T-shirt,' said Jimmy Pats. 'Padre Pio, he's your man. He was a great one for fighting the aliens. He single-handedly fought off an alien invasion in 1956, but the CIA covered it up. He was so traumatised by the whole experience, that he needed to get a haircut.'

'Ah, will ya get out of that, Jimmy Pats,' I said, 'next you'll be claiming that he invented Monopoly.'

'Do you know something, Johnny, your lack of religion is becoming an embarrassment. Hey, Enya, did you ever read that cool book by Padre Pio, the one called *The Agony in the Garden*?'

'Yeah,' said Enya, 'but I much preferred the one he wrote on the Immaculate Conception.'

While those two lunatics were talking about Padre Pio and aliens, I went over and sat next to Julie Hegarty. No sooner had I sat down than I realised it was a mistake. As I looked up I could see Padre Pio glaring down at me. He had this big silver cup in his hands and he looked like he was about to bring it down on my head. But that was only Enya's T-shirt. The worst thing was, Enya was *inside the T-shirt* and she was standing right over us.

'What are you doin' talking to my boyfriend?' said Enya to Julie.

'I ... I ... I never said a word to him,' pleaded Julie.

'Look, Enya, I just sat down next to her, for Heaven's sake. Look, you don't want to cause a scene – you're wearing a religious T-shirt.'

Enya looked at Julie, who at this stage was

trembling. I could see that Enya was trying to decide who to hit first, me or Julie, when suddenly I could hear Snots Murphy:

'Hey, Enya, what do you want to be? The boot or the wheelbarrow? Or if you want, you can be the dog.'

Now, of course, Snots was talking about what piece Enya wanted to play with on the Monopoly board. But Enya hadn't ever played Monopoly before, as she was more into contact sports, so she thought Snots was trying to insult her.

'Who are you callin' a dog, you little toe-rag?'

But Snots didn't get what was happening, so he just tried to be helpful. 'Well, Enya, if you're not the dog, you can be the boot.'

Enya picked Snots up by the two ears and lifted him three feet off the ground. For a second she looked a bit like Padre Pio lifting up that big silver cup.

Taking advantage of the fact that Enya's hands were full, Monkey Murphy decided to be brave:

'You leave Snots alone, you pimply-faced psycho-naut,' screamed Monkey, pulling Enya by one of her pigtails.

Enya dropped Snots onto the coffee table and chopped Monkey across the nose with her arm. In the next minute there was absolute chaos. Orla Daly, who's Monkey's girlfriend, was pulling Enya by the other pigtail, and Julie Hegarty had hidden behind the sofa. Snots was on the floor suffering from concussion and Jimmy Pats was running around like a lunatic, shouting, 'Mind the Monopoly board, you barbarians, it's the only one I've got.' Blister O'Flynn, being the wisest kid I know, just went to the jacks and locked the door.

As for me, I sat in my chair, watching the whole thing. By this time Enya had Orla Daly in a headlock and Monkey was upside-down in the fireplace. Jimmy Pats was running around trying to gather up his Monopoly money, and the money and little plastic houses and chance-cards were flying all over the place. Then a chance-card landed in my lap and I turned it over. It said: *Go Back Three Spaces ...*

the evil spirit of Homen Hotep ...

Well, to tell you the truth (and I mean the real truth now, not that stuff everybody lies about), I was kinda nervous about Enya coming to our rehearsal. We were doing a practice gig for our band, The Dead Crocodiles, and Enya had never heard us play before.

Anyway, at the moment that Enya turned up to our

rehearsal, Jimmy Pats Murphy was half-way through his guitar solo, and anyone with sensitive hearing would probably have gone into a coma as soon as they heard it, but Enya just looked at him as if he was playing *a banjo* or something.

Blister O'Flynn, our bass-guitarist and vocalist, then started into the second verse of our best song, *Bad Hedgehog*:

'*Bad Hedgehog Bad Hedgehog Bad Hedgehog*
Hedgehog gave
his spiky coat
to an old lady
who was cold
but first he turned
it inside out
so then
she died
Bad Hedgehog Bad Hedgehog Bad Hedgehog,'
sang Blister.

From behind the drum kit I was watching Enya very carefully. She looked at us without blinking an eye, and I thought to myself, *either we're better than I thought, or else she's gone deaf.*

After the session Enya came up and offered me a Tayto.

'Hey, Johnny, I liked that *Bad Hedeghog* song. I'm thinkin' of getting one as a pet. So, who writes yer lyrics?'

'Oh, that's me, Enya. I'm the chief poet of The Dead Crocodiles.'

'But, Johnny, I thought you *hated* poetry,' said Enya.

'Nah, I don't hate *real* poetry, only that poofy stuff by William Shakespeare and John Keats. Real poetry is cool.'

'Yeah, and you know something else, Johnny, I like the name of your band. Probably 'cos I got a crocodile of my own.'

'Yeah, well the thing is, we named the band after one of my favourite novels. You know, by that science-fiction writer, Shaughnessy-Shaughnessy O'Shaughnessy. Hey, Enya, it's a really cool book, you should read it. It starts off in ancient Egypt, and there's this High Priest called Homen Hotep, and he's killing all these people and stealing their hearts. He's cooking this enormous stew out of human insides, and it's boiling and boiling away for months in his cooking pot. It's for some kind of ancient spell that's gonna make him immortal. But the thing is, he can't let the pot dry out, 'cos that would break the spell, so he has to keep filling it with *more and more* human hearts. Now, after he's killed all these people he uses their dead bodies in his experiments, 'cos he's a real nutter, and he mixes their bodies up with the bodies of crocodiles, and he invents these kind of crocodile-men, which he uses as his slaves. And he starts to give himself some surgery, so he's one of the crocodile-men himself, like, he's the chief dude of the crocodile-men. Then he tries to take over Egypt and become dictator, but the Pharaoh defeats him and he gets captured. Now, the thing is, he's created about *fifty* of these crocodile people, and they're dangerous because they're going around eating everyone in sight, but the Pharaoh doesn't want to kill them because crocodiles are sacred to the Egyptians, and he's frightened that it might anger the crocodile gods. So he gets his magicians, and they cast a spell on Homen Hotep and the crocodile-men, which sends them into a deep sleep, and they get put into these crocodile-shaped mummy cases that are buried in the swamps near the River Nile. They stay in the swamps for thousands of years until they get discovered by modern-day archeologists, who take the mummy-cases to a museum in Cairo. Then the crocodile-people escape and start living in the sewers.'

'*Then* what do they do?' asked Enya.

'Ah, come on, Enya, get real! They start *eating people*, what do ya think they do?'

Enya said nothing for a few moments, but just kept munching at her Taytos. She seemed deep in thought. Then she said: 'Do you know something, Johnny, if you're reading books like this, no wonder you're writing such brilliant poetry. He sounds like an inspiration, Johnny, like a real inspiration. And do you know something else, Johnny? He's just inspired *me* as well.'

'How do you mean, Enya?'

'Well, Johnny, I've just realised what it is that The Dead Crocodiles need.'

'Yeah, you mean somebody that can really play lead-guitar?'

'No, Johnny, I mean *a manager*. And that manager's gonna be *me*. And The Dead Crocodiles are gonna conquer the world.'

Enya stood quietly. Her hair was done up at the front in an enormous orange spike and she looked like some kind of spotty unicorn. But as she left the hall I noticed her shadow against the wall. Her big spike of hair stood up in the shadows like the upright snout of a crocodile. And I thought, *oops*.

And I wasn't the *only one* who spotted her shadow. Jimmy Pats Murphy and Blister O'Flynn saw it as well.

'Do you know what *I* think, Johnny?' said Jimmy Pats, looking at Enya's departing shadow. 'I think this is a sign.'

'What, you mean like a sign from Heaven?'

'Nah, Johnny. A sign from ancient *Egypt*.'

Yeah, it looked like we had a new manager. And it looked like our new manager was the evil dead spirit of *Homen Hotep*. Yep, things for The Dead Crocodiles could only get better.

we'll make a fortune ...

Anyway, we got a call to go around to Enya's. Jimmy Pats, Blister O'Flynn and myself. So we call around and Enya's brother opens the door. Now, for the first time in my life I couldn't say with any certainty that Enya's brother had snots over his face. On account of the fact that his face was completely covered *in black ink*!

'Now, be careful and don't make a mess,' said Enya's brother, 'cos der house is nearly tidy and Enya might resign as yer manager.'

As he walked through the hall, we could see that the soles of his shoes were also covered in black ink, and he left a trail of his footprints all over the carpet. I also noticed that a big blob of sellotape was stuck to the back of his hair, as well as a lump of week-old chewing gum. Hey, I'd never seen him looking so tidy.

Anyway, when we get into the kitchen, there's Enya by the table, and she's cutting the sleeves off of these manky old T-shirts. And, man, when I say manky, I mean *manky*. There was bacteria on them that could kill the whole of China.

But on the other side of the table were these kind of cream-coloured T-shirts that looked sort of weird, as if they'd had radiation-treatment or something. Enya's brother was taking these ones, one by one, and stamping them with a stencil that was shaped like a crocodile. He was covering the stencil each time in black ink from a roller, and although he was covered in black ink from head to toe, he was printing the T-shirts so carefully, it was unbelievable.

'Hey, kid, you're doin' a great job with the T-shirts,' I said.

'Yeah, Enya says I can get as much ink on me as I like, as long as I'm careful with der T-shirts. It's great!!'

It was then I noticed that the T-shirts he was printing on had their sleeves cut off as well.

'Don't worry, Johnny,' announced Enya, 'these manky ones are goin' into the washing machine with bleach, so they come out clean but dingy. The reason I'm cutting off the sleeves is to make them look mean. These are gonna be our Dead Crocodiles merchandise. We'll make a fortune.'

Well, I looked down at the dingy creamy T-shirts with the black crocodiles printed on them, and quite frankly, I didn't think anyone in their right mind would buy one. That was until I tried one on.

'Hey, Johnny,' said Jimmy Pats, 'that's a *cool* T-shirt, even if it *was* designed by two psychopaths.'

Within a minute even Blister O'Flynn had one on.

'So, Enya, how much are you gonna sell these things for?' I asked.

'Well, Johnny, I get them in the charity shop for 50p each. After I've bleached them and shrunk them, so that they all fit the average twelve-year-old, we can sell them for two pounds.'

Now, what I didn't realise was that she had *fifty* of these things.

'Enya, are you mad or what? How could you spend twenty-five pounds on this utter rubbish?'

'Ah, Johnny, you're such a dork. They were only rubbish when I bought them. Now that I've bleached them and printed crocodiles on them they're top quality merchandise.'

as a band we were absolute crap ...

So, on the Saturday Enya organised our first gig at the youth centre. Admission was free, which was a relief, because people actually turned up. Enya stood at the front door with her pet crocodile tied around the neck by a piece of skipping-rope. She was wearing a Dead Crocodiles T-shirt and a pair of black leather pants. By a table just inside the door was her brother with a pile of T-shirts in front of him. For an extra pound you could lie face-down on the ground. Then Enya would put some black ink on the crocodile's foot and the crocodile would stand on you and you'd have a croc footprint on the back of your T-Shirt. You'd also get most of the bones in your body crushed to pieces. It was obvious that nobody would go for it, but the thing was, *everybody* went for it.

Now, I'm gonna be perfectly honest and say that as a band we were absolute crap. Jimmy Pats Murphy outdid himself as the worst guitarist in the whole world, and even managed to blow all the electric sockets in the entire building. Snots Murphy, who was acting as our roadie, succeeded in getting the lights back on, but not without first electrocuting himself six times. All of his hair fell out and his bogies glowed in the dark. And Blister O'Flynn, not to be outdone, forgot the words to most of our songs. As for the drumming, well, what can I say? Even the best drummer in the whole world has a bad day. And of course, not many people actually managed to dance, on account of the fact that they were hindered by broken bones and internal bleeding, courtesy of the crocodile.

But the night wasn't a total disaster. Enya's crocodile spent the remainder of the evening chasing Monkey Murphy around the hall. Monkey still has one of the crocodile's teeth as a souvenir. But nobody is allowed to see it, as it's still stuck in his bum.

And the best thing is, we sold every single one of those T-shirts. Which means we made £75, plus the extra £50 we made from the croc footprints. *I* was happy. *Enya* was happy. Even Enya's *crocodile* was happy.

Yeah, who needs to be any good at rock 'n' roll, when all you have to do is sell *T-shirts*?

THE
Dead Crocodiles

ACKNOWLEDGEMENTS

I would like to thank Batman, The Purple Claw, The Green Lantern, The Creeper, The Doom Patrol, The Justice League, Dr Strange, The X-Men, Prince Namor, The Fantastic Four, Spiderman, The Vision, Antman, The Lone Ranger, Captain Scarlet, Tarzan, Marine Boy, Adam Adamant, King Kong and Cordwainer Bird. Not only did these god-like creatures strike fear into the hearts of evil-doers everywhere, but they also expanded my mind sufficently to enable me to eventually become a writer.

The Johnny Coffin Diaries originally saw life as a chapter-by-chapter insert in my radio programme ***The Ivory Tower***. Many people helped coax, encourage and influence me during the extended period of writing. However, there would have been no Johnny Coffin whatsoever if it had not been for the poet Mary O'Malley. On a Friday night in December, 1998, Mary O'Malley and I gave a poetry reading as part of that year's ***Bricín Winter Arts Festival*** in Killarney. On the following Monday I received a 'phone call from Jacqui Corcoran, a producer at RTE, who said that Mary had recommended me and had suggested that I might be good at writing for radio. As a result of this totally unselfish act of faith in my abilities, there began a fruitful collaborative relationship with Jacqui Corcoran, who was to become my producer on several projects. Indeed, Jacqui's faith in me was equal only to Mary's, and no writer could wish for a more perfect collaborator.

Words on a page are words on a page, but on radio those words have to be brought to life. I want to thank Jack Doyle Ryan for turning Johnny Coffin into a real kid, and for convincing the entire country that he really existed. Because of Jack he really did exist. I would also like to thank Sam Ryan, Jack's brother, who came on board and acted in the show, and their mother Dots Ryan for letting them play in the nuthouse. Many other actors and performers helped bring the programme to life. Sean Corcoran, who plays not only Professor Bang, but also Mr Darkness and Mr McCluskey, is a true Cosmic Surfer who deserves to take his place upon the Mountain of Eternity, and one day I'm sure he will. I'd also like to thank Leona Daly, Richard Hourigan (yes, Richard, even you), Dominic Moore, Shiela Penkert,

Joe Meagher, David Deegan, Eileen Sheehan, James Corcoran Hodgins a.k.a. Baby Bang and his granny Dee Corcoran, who all performed in the programme at various times.

Lots of people helped give me ideas and support. My wife Jenny puts up with all the nonsense of being married to a writer, and one day she'll end up in heaven with all the angels. And if she's very lucky I won't be up there with her. In the early days of the programme, when I was trying to get inside the mind of a small schoolboy, my youngest son Gerard gave me a zillion ideas. Thanks, son.

The Fia Rua Writers' Group in Killarney helped stimulate the brain cells. Some individuals deserve a special mention. Neil Bedford for answering the 'phone. Marion Moynihan for being herself. Margaret O'Shea and her husband Paul, and their son Small Paul (who, oddly, is over six foot tall), for welcoming me into their home and giving me some of my best lines. For Mike and Eileen Sheehan and their rather extensive family, which seems to increase and decrease at will, containing as it does many waifs and strays, for allowing me to be one of those waifs and strays. Their cat Ginger, for eating goldfish. Michèle Vassal, Brendan, Marjolaine and Eimhín, for cooking an Anti-Matter Chocolate Cake. Anthony McGuinness for being my sometime collaborator, and his wife, Patricia. And Nelly Flynn, for being my weirdo friend.

Finally, I would like to thank Mary Webb, my editor at The O'Brien Press. Long after the book was finished she came up with a brilliant idea that I quite happily stole and put into the final chapter. And now it's mine.

OTHER BOOKS FROM THE O'BRIEN PRESS

FROM EOIN COLFER

BENNY AND OMAR

Benny, a young sports fanatic, is forced to leave his beloved Wexford, home of all his hurling heroes, and move with his family to Tunisia! How will he survive in a place like this – they've never even *heard* of the All Ireland! Then he teams up with Omar, and a madcap friendship between the two boys leads to trouble, crazy escapades, a unique way of communicating and heartbreaking challenges.

Paperback £5.50/€6.95/$7.95

BENNY AND BABE

Benny's back – large as life and twice as troublesome! Benny and his family are home again and visiting Grandfather in the country. Benny's position as a 'townie' makes him the object of much teasing by the natives. Babe is the village tomboy, given serious respect by the all the local tough guys. She runs a thriving business and just might consider Benny as her business partner. But things become very complicated, and dangerous, when Furty Howlin also wants a slice of the action.

Paperback £4.99/€6.34/$7.95

THE WISH LIST

Meg Finn is in trouble. Unearthly trouble. Cast out of her own home by her stepfather after her mother's death, Meg gets mixed up with thieving Belch and ends up in a very sticky situation. Meg's soul is up for grabs as the divine and the demonic try every underhanded ploy imaginable to claim it. Her only chance for salvation is the pensioner she wronged. And even if she manages the impossible, will she really have enough good points to face up to St Peter?

An unforgettable and gritty tale of life, death and an unexpected hereafter.

Paperback £4.99/€6.34/$7.95

FROM CREINA MANSFIELD

MY NASTY NEIGHBOURS

David and his family are typical: three messy, noisy teenagers; two tidy, organised parents. It just doesn't work, does it? But when Mum inherits some money, they finally hit on a solution – buy the house next door. Now they can live separate lives – teens in number 8 and parents in number 10. At first it seems like paradise, but then things begin to go wrong …

Paperback £4.99/€6.34/$7.95

CHEROKEE

Gene's grandfather, Cherokee, is a famous jazz musician and Gene travels the world with him. He loves the life and his only ambition is to be a musician, too. But Aunt Joan is totally opposed to the idea. When Gene is left behind on an island by accident, she seizes her chance to give him a 'normal' life, away from Cherokee's influence. Is this the end of Gene's dreams, and what is really behind his aunt's resentment of Cherokee and his lifestyle? Escape seems the only answer – but life has a lot of surprises in store for Gene.

Paperback £5.47/€6.95/$7.95

FROM GREGORY MAGUIRE

SEVEN SPIDERS SPINNING

Seven baby Siberian snow spiders, frozen since the Ice Age, defrost on their way to a science lab. They wake up in a wood where the Tattletales girls' club are planning for the school Hallowe'en Horror Pageant. Their goal is to wipe the floor with their arch-enemies, the Copycats – all boys, naturally. For the spiders, it's love at first sight. One by one, each of the tarantulas finds its way to its own chosen Tattletale. But, as each one fails to return, the other spiders become sadder, and madder. So when the final three reach the school, they're looking for love at first Bite!

Paperback £3.99/€5.07